3 4028 07628 6732
HARRIS COUNTY PUBLIC LIBRARY

J Boos
Boos, Ben
Fa   istic realm
P9-CNE-152
$19.99
ocn502029782
1st ed.   02/07/2011

FANTASY

To my mother and father

Copyright © 2010 by Ben Boos

All rights reserved. No part of this book may be reproduced, transmitted, or stored in an information retrieval system in any form or by any means, graphic, electronic, or mechanical, including photocopying, taping, and recording, without prior written permission from the publisher.

First edition 2010

Library of Congress Cataloging-in-Publication Data is available.

Library of Congress Catalog Card Number 2010007511

ISBN 978-0-7636-4056-9

10 11 12 13 14 15 16 SCP 10 9 8 7 6 5 4 3 2 1

Printed in Humen, Dongguan, China

This book was typeset in Historical Fell.
The illustrations were done in digital media.

Candlewick Press
99 Dover Street
Somerville, Massachusetts 02144

visit us at www.candlewick.com

FANTASY

AN ARTIST'S REALM

WRITTEN & ILLUSTRATED BY

BEN BOOS

CANDLEWICK PRESS

:: Author's Note ::

When I was a boy, I used to sketch and doodle to escape boredom
and, well, just to escape. Deskbound in body, I could wander far,
far away — and I learned that a mind can wander where it will;
no walls can stop it!

On one occasion, I recall sketching some big, ominous-looking
doors with bulky iron hinges twisted into gnarly shapes. I wished I
was creating a door to another place — a place full of strange cities,
green fields, giant mountains, and deep, dark forests. There would
be monsters, treasure, and ample adventure. I remember staring at
that illustrated door when I was done, pretending there was an entire
world beyond its threshold.

I've revisited this old idea to recapture some of the boyish wonder
that haunts me, even after all these years. Here is my hand-drawn
"door" to another place, inspired by endless daydreams and the light
of many minds. I hope you enjoy it, and may it aid you in your own
adventures and escapes!

Travel well, friend, in both real life and fantasy.

Ben Boos

:: Contents ::

The Magic Door

A Partial Map of New Perigord

PART I

*On exploring and finding some notable inhabitants
of the land called New Perigord*

PART II

*On travel beyond the fields of man, and the presence
of non-human societies*

PART III

*On the dangers of the Black Perigord and its vast tracts
of wasteland and wilderness*

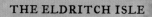

THE ELDRITCH ISLE

ELVES
AND
FAIRIES

THE GREEN PERIGORD REGION

THE EAST MOORS

THE NESSA
RIVER

THE MEADOWLANDS

ROGUES
AND
THIEVES

DWARVES

DWARVE
MINE:

LAKE AMAIA

THE ELDERBRIAR
FOREST

RED PERIGORD REGION

THE STRAI
STORFI

THE CLARISSANT SEA

SKELLIG

MAGES
AND
ADEPTS

NORTHBURREN

PALADINS

THE
CITY OF
GALLIENE

THE ORIANNA RIVER

CAER-DUNMORE

FIGHTERS

TO THE IMPERIAL
CITIES OF THE WEST

THE GRAY PERIGORD REGION

THE LONG VELDT

CAER-AELISH

A PARTIAL MAP OF

NEW PERIGORD

NOT TO SCALE

CLERICS
AND
HEALERS

TO THE WOLF PLAINS

BEWARE ALL

WHO ENTER HERE

THE PASS
OF GIANTS

THE FROSTMARCH TUNDRA

THE BAY
OF EELS

THE WASTE

THE RUINS OF
GRYPHONSPERCH

THE EXOTIC CITIES OF THE EAST

DRAGONS, GIANTS, AND
OTHER BEASTS

THE SEA OF DUST

THE KALISATRA MOUNTAINS

THE SABLE DESERT

TO THE JUNGLES OF THE SOUTH

THE BURNED LAND

THE SILVERNAIL
MOUNTAINS

MINOTAURS

THE MOUNTAIN
OF ASH

THE BORDERLANDS

HOBGOBLINS

THISTLETOP
CASTLE

THE WATCHTOWERS
OF GRAY OAK

THE LONELY ROAD

LICHES
AND THE
UNDEAD

THE BLACK PERIGORD REGION

THE NECROPOLIS

THE TOWER
DUNGEON OF SERYU

THE BLACK FENS

THE CAMELWOOD FORES

FELL CREATURES

THE IRONBELT
MOUNTAINS

THE ACID BASIN

PART I

HAIL, STRANGER, AND WELCOME!

Choose a sturdy walking stick and a warm and comfortable cloak, and prepare for adventure! There are beautiful sights here and treasures to be found by the bold and the curious. May the roads of this land be open to you, and may the folk treat you kindly. But, alas, it is not a realm without adversity, so keep your blades sharp and your armor fitted well.

Most visitors to this continent will have come from across the sea and will likely arrive in the tamer lands of the Gray Perigord region. This is just as well; one can get into trouble enough among the hedgerows and fields of the West.

The Paladins, with their buttressed fortifications, offer a measure of calm from the rigors of the field, and their territory is a good place to start exploring. Brigands shy from the places where Paladins gather and hold dominion, and even the wolves and bears of the forest are less of a threat in this cultivated territory.

One of the finest places of the Holy Paladin knights is that bastion town called Northburren. There, the comrades of the watch can give out excellent and generous advice about travel in New Perigord.

NORTHBURREN

Beyond the domesticated countryside around Northburren, one will quickly find that the landscape reverts to the province of the hunter, fisherman, and woodcutter — thickets and brambles lead to hinterlands of primeval forest, and many of the emerald groves open up to the barrens, bogs, and wild moors that are so dangerous to traverse. Stick to the roads and trails, unless you have the intrepid wanderlust of an adventurer combined with well-honed survival skills.

THE WILDS OF THE GRAY PERIGORD REGION

Nestled in the viridian mountains of the Gray Perigord region, the enclave of Skellig overlooks the Clarissant Sea and the ruddy delta waters of the Nessa River. Here, in this remote and unlikely place, is a library of the ancients as well as the schools of magic that draw hungry learners like moths to a flame.

SKELLIG

If you wish to travel to Skellig to imbibe of its knowledge or hire one of its many eminent mages, there is a cave passage that leads directly into the wizardly compound. This passage is at the end of the old coastal road, in the east moors, and it can save one a dangerous climb through mountain wilderness.

The password for entry is "SAPIENTIA."

The continent of New Perigord is divided into four regions: the Gray Perigord, where humankind dwells; the Red Perigord, which is home to the dwarven race; the Green Perigord of the fairy folk; and the foul place called the Black Perigord, where all manner of evil breeds. That is not to say that dangers are limited to the Black region; dangers seem to find their way into every corner of the map.

The Paladins fight to hold the northwestern portion of the Gray region, and a varied assemblage of professional fighters keeps order in the southwest areas. These fighters are lodged in a series of rugged barracks and forts, which the emperor has placed strategically to withstand the onslaughts of invading armies and creatures.

One such imperial fort is called Caer-Dunmore, home to some of the finest soldiers and destriers for leagues around.

CAER-DUNMORE

Though such forts as Caer-Dunmore do not offer much in the way of luxurious lodging, they can feed and water any mounts and will freely put up travelers in their simple yet spacious dormitories.

If you need rest and recuperation or the curing of wounds or ailments, then the monastery of Caer-Aelish, located on the Orianna River, is the choice destination. The infirmary there is tended by first-class clerics and healers.

CAER-AELISH

The scenic monastery of Caer-Aelish is situated near a wildwood forest known as the Elderbriar, which serves as a plentiful source of botanical healing ingredients.

Many forest-dwelling druids and wise women live within the lush vales and ancient groves of the Elderbriar. They make a fine living by trading plants, tinctures, and healing potions to the monks, clerics, and battlefield surgeons of the nearby monastery.

THE CAPITAL CITY OF GALLIENE

The gem of New Perigord, the capital city of Galliene, is a huge and thriving metropolis. Placed between two major rivers and the massive Lake Amaia, it is a perfect center for trade and export. It is also the emperor's westernmost foothold in the Perigords and a source of much pride. Mind you, it does not rival the cities of the Far West for sheer size, or the distant tower cities of the Southern Caliphates for pure opulence, but no other city in the empire attracts more exotic and quality trade. Its bustling harbor is a prime moneymaker for the emperor, and is thus jealously guarded.

Galliene is home to some of the toughest fighting folk in all the world, but it is also home to the quiet rogues of the local Thieves' Guild. These wolfish maidens and men of the shadows dwell wherever there is a busy harbor or the hustle and bustle of trade. The rogues dominate the "maze," which is a network of canal streets, catwalks, alleys, and huddled shops out of sight of the cobbled promenades, open lanes, and, of course, the city watch. If you must contact the Thieves' Guild for your own reasons, you might want to inquire with the barkeep at the Hog's Tooth tavern, in the heart of the Fishermen's Quarter.

CHAPTER 1
PALADINS

If you wander the misty coasts of the Northwest long enough, you are likely to come across the forts and bastions of the Paladins. Their spires stab the clouds — beckoning and welcoming from afar. These noble warriors bring a luminous fury into battle, and when they ride united, they strike deep terror into the heart of evil. The Paladins are few in number, but none are better suited than they to combat demons and other devilish manifestations.

The Paladin is a being of high oaths and shining steel, and his most cherished weapon is the sword.

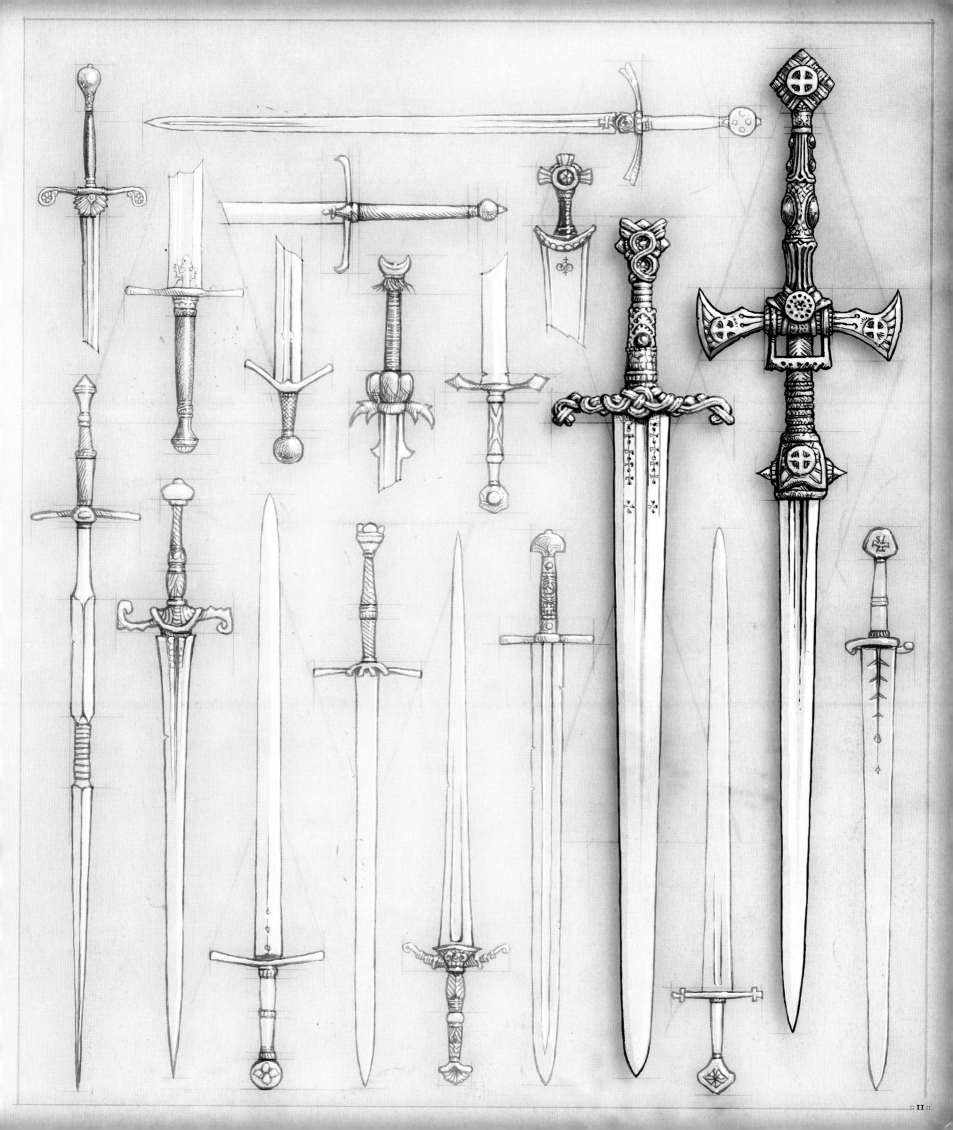

When the Paladins are not engaged in military campaigns, they are usually brooding, studying, or holding council from their estates. But they are also often called away on strange missions and far travel out of the blue. They are known to gather suddenly and to depart just as quickly: from their various strongholds, they just up and away, by warhorse, ship, or foot.

Becoming a Paladin

Some join the Paladins first as squires, seeking to be dubbed knights after a time of learning and service. Others, by the serendipity of life, are gifted by the chance and destiny of a sudden calling, and they are, on occasion, welcomed immediately into the highest ranks of the Order. The path of training for the Paladins is unique: they are creatures of battle, yet they seem to dedicate little study to combat. Instead, their fighting prowess seems to be almost meta-physical and inspired — it just arises within them, like an emanation. When they are called upon by the Fates to show heart and bravery, it almost seems as if they fight with a guided hand.

Paladin Estates

The Paladins share a portion of their bounty with a small army of craftsmen, builders, farmers, swordsmiths, and armorers who labor under the Paladin banner. Paladins are noted for keeping only the finest artisans, despite the high cost. They can afford this, since the war chests of the Order are always filled with the gifts of those who seek help against the privations caused by dragons, giants, vampires, demons, and such lot.

Quests and Secrecy

Why the Paladins sojourn in the wildest places and why they risk the perils of the oceans in their daring quests and explorations none can say. They keep such business strictly to themselves.

The Paladins of Northburren

Northburren is a Paladin outpost on the coast of the Clarissant Sea in that region called the Gray Perigord. It stands upon a dangerous frontier where the Paladins offer a much-needed source of protection and stability. In fact, the local knights maintain an active seaport as well as profitable estates and vineyards. The armory also houses some distinguished relic weapons, which bring no small amount of fame to Northburren.

Relic Swords

Relic swords are blessed by the holiest waters and the tears of sages. They are made with fragments taken from the most sacred and secret of reliquaries.

Ancient scrolls suggest that certain relic weapons were forged from parts of the swords of the Archangels themselves, who cast aside their broken blades after the ancient war of binding. If it is true that pieces of the four Elemental Blades were recovered and kept after all these countless millennia, then that would help explain the power behind some of these artifacts. Evil minions positively hate them, and even smaller devils go out of their way to avoid them.

This much is certain: if the remaining demons of the Lost Houses manage to reassemble a horde to march against the cities of humankind as they did of old, then the relic swords of the Paladins will be sorely needed.

Swords of the Archangels

When the Seraphim waged a war of banishment upon the Major Demons at the beginning of the age, they did so with wondrous and terrible weapons, including the Elemental Swords of the Archangels. Legend claims that these weapons were destroyed by a final clash with the demons, causing continents to sink and several stars to go dark in the sky as the swords shattered.

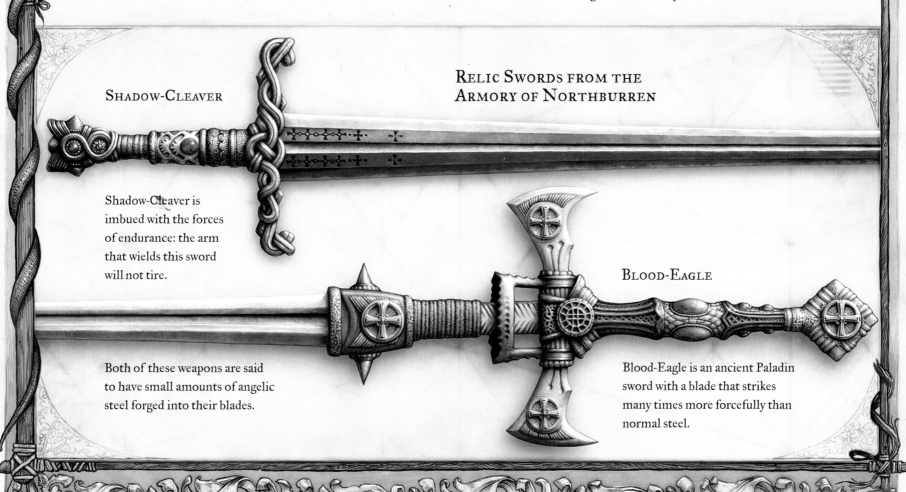

Relic Swords from the Armory of Northburren

Shadow-Cleaver

Shadow-Cleaver is imbued with the forces of endurance: the arm that wields this sword will not tire.

Both of these weapons are said to have small amounts of angelic steel forged into their blades.

Blood-Eagle

Blood-Eagle is an ancient Paladin sword with a blade that strikes many times more forcefully than normal steel.

A PALADIN FIGHTING A DEMON

CHAPTER 2 — MAGES & ADEPTS

The mind that can comprehend the vastness of eternity can be wielded as a weapon. Mages and sorcerers the world over have used strict disciplines of learning to focus and train their minds. This learning is carefully kept and passed on in the various schools and academies of learning and wizardry.

But magic is not a path for the weak-willed, for with power comes responsibility — and the forces of balance will ever hound the careless magic user. Only a soul that can walk the razor's edge of learning and self-control is a true Adept.

THE STUDY & PERFECTION
OF THE MYSTICAL ARTS

SCHOOLS OF MAGIC

The secrets of making and unmaking, which give the magic user his power, are the product of both intellect and intuition, which is to say that one's natural gifts can be honed by the rigors of study and discipline.

There are many kinds of magic, from the plant spells of the wrinkled *curanderos* to the star readings of the northern ascetics. There are also many teachers and masters of the arcane arts. Some are scattered throughout the loneliest places on the map, while others congregate, as do the mages, in the town of Skellig. That enclave in particular is home to many academies of learning and is highly recommended as a starting place for any aspiring magician. The towering libraries of Skellig are second to none.

BECOMING AN ADEPT

Every Neophyte dreams of achieving the ascendant qualities of the Adept. To become an Adept is to become a master of the arts of magic — able to do with precision what a lesser mage would botch.

The Adept is a mage in total control of his or her mind. Such a one can weave the very fabric of becoming — like lightning from the fingertips — without destroying mind or body.

The path to becoming an Adept is unique for every mage and depends in part on the branch of magic that one attempts to master. Few will actually attain the title, but those who do are incredible forces to contend with, whether they be alchemists crafting magic items or true mages-of-war.

TELEKINESIS AND LEVITATION

Sages of the metaphysical arts tell us that all things are connected by a web of energy that most cannot see. By mentally engaging with this energy, or "ether," a mage can move and levitate even heavy objects. This can be achieved because the space between objects is subject to alteration by the perception mechanics of a magic user.

An Enchantress levitates a heavy chest by manipulating the ethereal powers.

According to legend, the levitation magic of hundreds of mages was used in the construction of the great Minotaur labyrinths of the East as well as in the deep, deep catacombs under the Necropolis, in the Black Perigord.

COMMON SPELLS OF UTILITY AND DEFENSE

LEVITATE: Invokes an ethereal lifting force that is directed by the caster's mind.

MAGIC CIRCLE: Casts a circle of banishing for demons and evil spirits.

MAGIC GLOW: A simple spell that creates a floating orb of light.

DISTANT SIGHT: Gives the caster a glimpse of a remote location.

ETHER SHIELD: Conjures energy armor, which can block physical attacks.

COMMON SPELLS OF COMBAT

PARALYZE: This spell sends an immobilizing shock of ether force to an enemy.

FIRE ARROW: Shoots an arrowlike projectile of burning ether magic from the caster's hands.

FIRE WIND: Similar to Fire Arrow, but this spell sends entire sheets and gusts of flame.

ICE JAVELIN: A mental concentration of the ether that can be frozen and hurled like a spear of ice.

LIGHTNING BOLT: A destructive bolt of energy that arcs from the caster to the chosen target.

EXAMPLES OF MAGICAL TOOLS
These are used to focus, store, and discharge magic energy.

THE STAFF OF PERCEPTION: Improves the user's sight.

A scroll of ancient ice spells

WAND OF FIRE
Ignites and casts forth a blast of fire at the will of the user. It has lit without fail for twelve generations.

WAND OF LIGHT
Radiates an aura that repulses evil things within a certain radius from the caster.

AMULET OF PROTECTION
Prevents arrows from hitting the wearer.

TALISMAN OF THE WILD
Allows communication with animals.

POTIONS OF VITALITY
These regenerate ethereal energy.

GRIMOIRES AND MAGIC BOOKS
Are full of secret formulas of divination and powerful spells.

MAGIC DAGGERS
These can penetrate almost any armor.

CANDLES AND INCENSE
These are enchanted to help focus the mind.

Those who can gain competence in magic are always sought during wars. Magic can tip the scales toward victory as well as any siege weapon, and thus a mage-of-war will be paid handsomely.

THE TOOLS OF A MAGE

CHAPTER 3

FIGHTERS

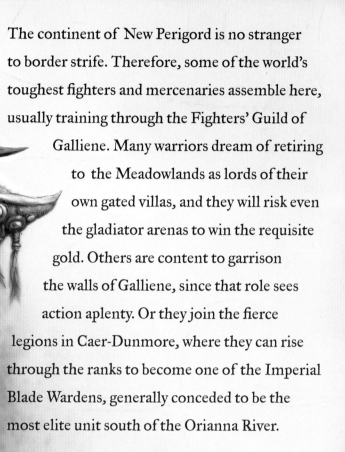

The continent of New Perigord is no stranger to border strife. Therefore, some of the world's toughest fighters and mercenaries assemble here, usually training through the Fighters' Guild of Galliene. Many warriors dream of retiring to the Meadowlands as lords of their own gated villas, and they will risk even the gladiator arenas to win the requisite gold. Others are content to garrison the walls of Galliene, since that role sees action aplenty. Or they join the fierce legions in Caer-Dunmore, where they can rise through the ranks to become one of the Imperial Blade Wardens, generally conceded to be the most elite unit south of the Orianna River.

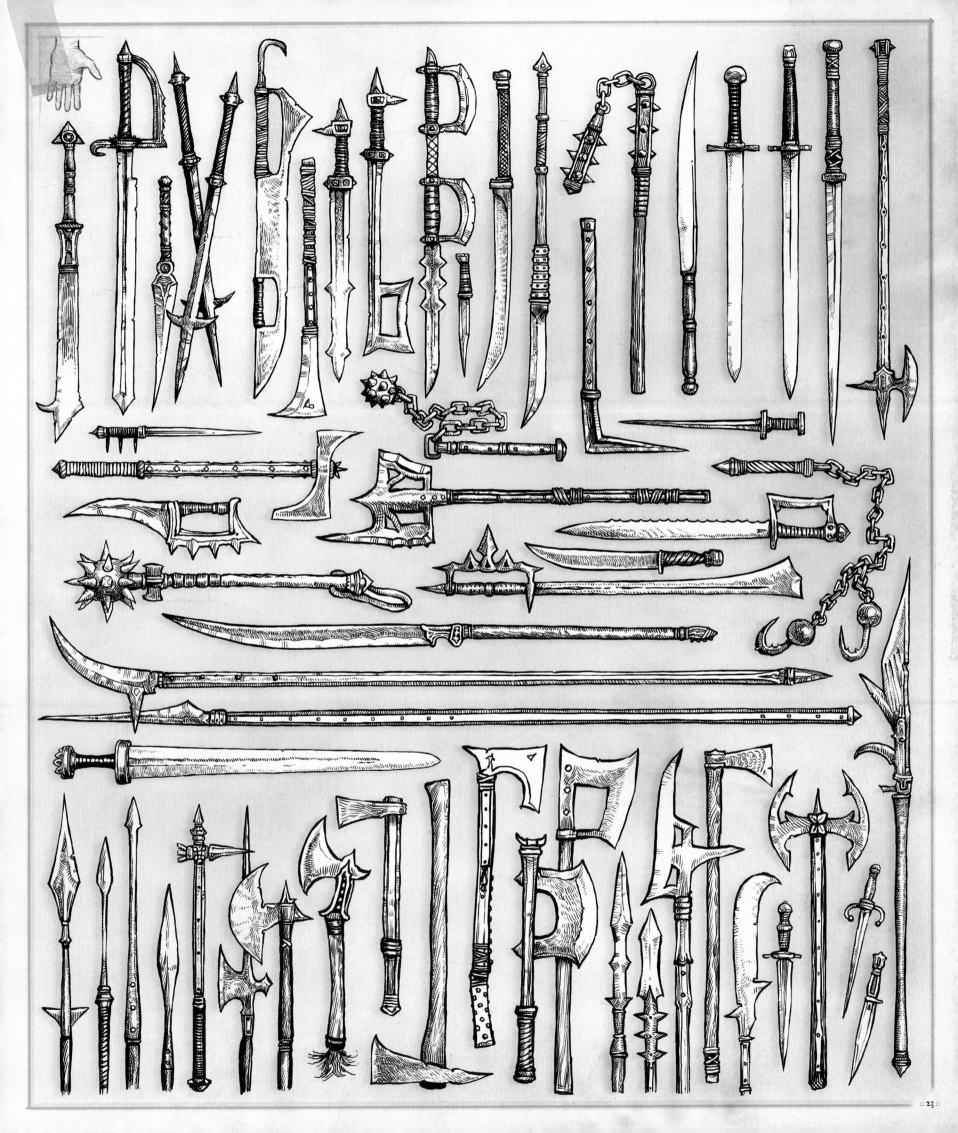

THE ARMORED LEGIONS

Caer-Dunmore is the northernmost military fortress of the empire. The riders of the Long Veldt are stationed there, along with infantry and some light auxiliary forces. Several hundred Imperial Blade Wardens use the fortress as a base of operations, including the squads lent to the Archon of Galliene. Farther north, the Paladins bravely extend the hand of order, but as everyone in the Gray Perigord knows, the strange wilds are all too near. . . .

The wars of the West occupy much of the attention of the hardened fighters of the Legion in Caer-Dunmore, but the wilderness must be ever watched. Steel is kept especially sharp, for plagues of the undead, swarms of fell creatures, hobgoblin invasions, and all manner of wicked assaults may occur from time to time. For proof, one need only look at the scarred and blackened walls of Galliene.

WEAPONS FOR THE FIGHTER

Melee Weapons
One can buy serviceable swords, axes, and spears in any village of the empire, but Galliene prides itself as a true center of the weapon-crafting art. It is no boast to say that war tools of every sort are available in the Smiths' Quarter in Galliene.

Ranged Weapons
These are the specialty of the fletchers and woodworkers, who turn out everything from small hand bows to the immense recurved foot bows of the Archon's palace guard.

Siege Weapons
The siegeworks, found along the north wall of Galliene, can provision a fighting unit with exceptional custom catapults, ballistas, and any other crew-manned weapons fighters could wish for.

ARMORERS' ROW: New Perigord is brimming with interesting trade and commerce, which brings exotic materials within the reach of the professional fighter. Elfin textiles and dwarven metals are only the beginning of what one can find in Armorers' Row in Galliene.

TYPES OF ARMOR: The suits of armor depicted below illustrate some of the more common types that are readily available. Magic armor and ancient specimens are omitted, as they are too complex to be covered here.

Quilted Armor: Light, flexible, and tough, this is a very common and affordable form of armor, worn by itself or as padding underneath other kinds of armor. The sort made with giant-worm silk is the best.

Leather Armor: Leather armor is also light, and yet, if made of *Baryonyx* hide or kraken skin, it can be almost as tough as any other sort of armor.

Scale Mail: Most scale mail is made of metal scales, which offer excellent protection from sharp weapons, but the varieties made with actual dragon scales are resistant to flame and heat as well.

FIGHTING SCHOOLS

Most military outposts will train a willing soldier, but if you wish to learn the finer skills of fighting, seek out the Fighters' Guild halls, which offer training in martial arts.

THE FIGHTERS' GUILD: The freelance fighters and bounty hunters of New Perigord have built up a loosely connected network of guildhalls throughout the empire. For a reasonable fee, they will assist with combat training and lodging. They also have great connections to the armorers and smiths, so that a fighter can get his gear fixed or maintained at a reasonable price.

Chain Mail: This armor is great at stopping a piercing point or a cutting blade but is less effective at buffering the crushing impact of an enemy strike. Commonly used under other armor.

Imperial Banded Armor: Favored by the emperor's troops and the riders of the Long Veldt, this armor offers a great mix of protective attributes. It is something of a hybrid, made with cloth, hardwood, and bands of metal.

Plate Mail: Full plate or partial plate mail is the heaviest but also generally the most protective armor against the all-out punishment of war. It is especially cherished by frontline fighters and shock troops.

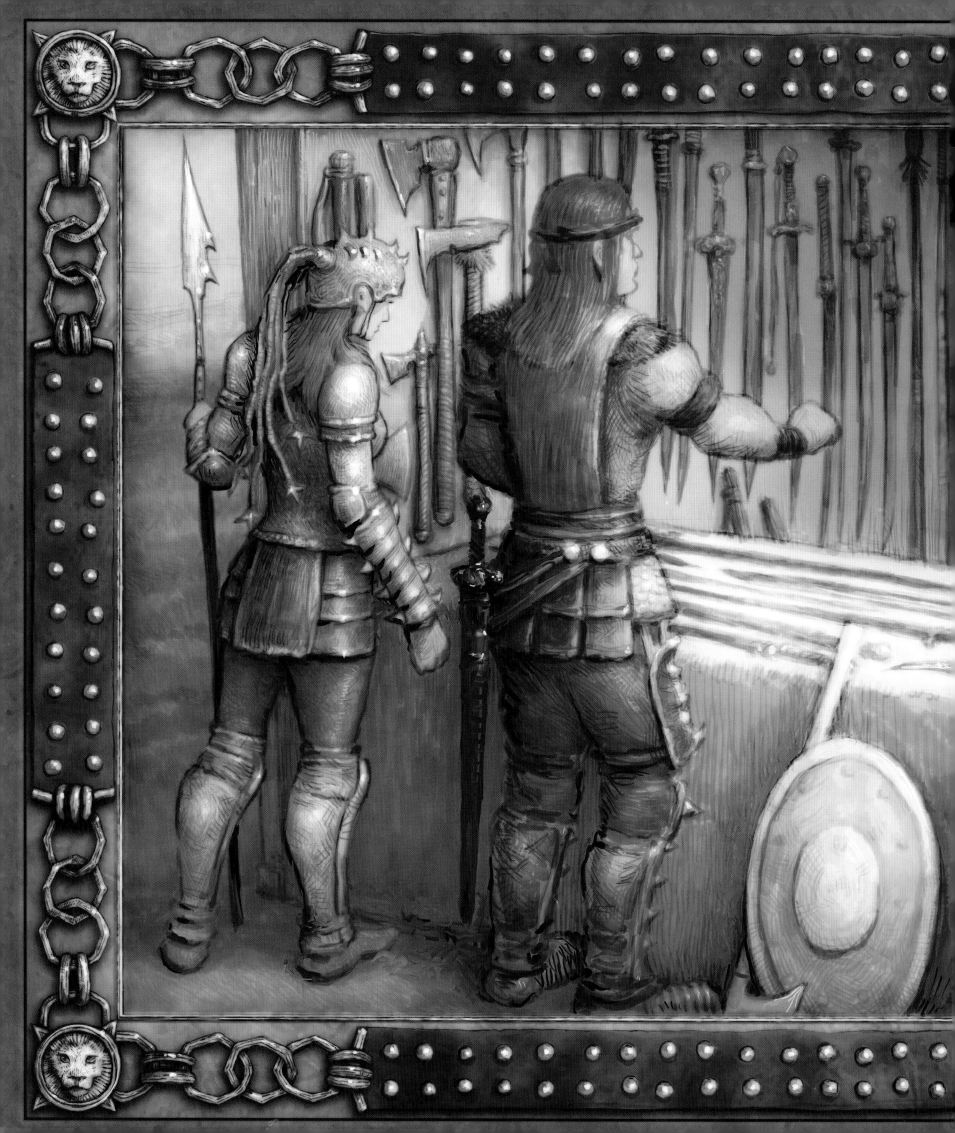

THE PROFFER OF A SILVER
COIN MIGHT CONVINCE A
WEAPON MERCHANT TO
SHOW YOU HIS FINER WARES,
USUALLY KEPT OUT OF SIGHT.

CHAPTER 04

CLERICS & HEALERS

Of those who choose to walk the path of learning, magic, and the arcane, there are certain individuals who devote themselves to the art of healing. They commit to the force of life, thereby using its natural energy to mend bones and heal wounds. That is not to say they will not fight when the situation demands — many are, in fact, experienced ex-soldiers and veteran explorers. Sometimes they have the most harrowing stories to tell about combat, battle, and war. Almost any fighting troop worth its salt keeps a cleric near at hand to aid in the aftermath of battle, and even the toughest adventurers are happy to call them company.

These brave souls go by many names and titles — clerics, white witches, monks, priests, and priestesses — yet, in essence, they all pursue the same paradigm of healing.

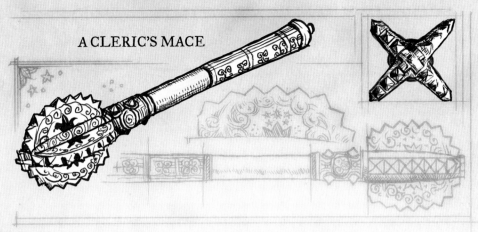

A CLERIC'S MACE

The mace is the traditional weapon of choice for many clerics. Though it may lack a cutting edge like a sword or ax, it can immobilize an enemy with equal aplomb. Many clerics are skilled at disabling an enemy without damage to vital nerves and arteries. After all, broken bones can be set and will heal with ease, as any benevolent cleric will tell you.

The scepterlike mace can also be used peacefully, for bestowing blessings or focusing healing energies. Further, it is a symbol of authority, natural law, and divine strength — fitting for this brave and distinguished class of people.

Bludgeoning weapons come in a remarkable number of shapes and sizes. A poor cleric who has disavowed material wealth might prefer a simple club, while clerics of high station may carry opulent scepters of silver and gold. If a healer is slight in stature, he or she can still fight effectively with a light mace, while a cleric of great strength may choose to heft a heavy maul or massive war hammer.

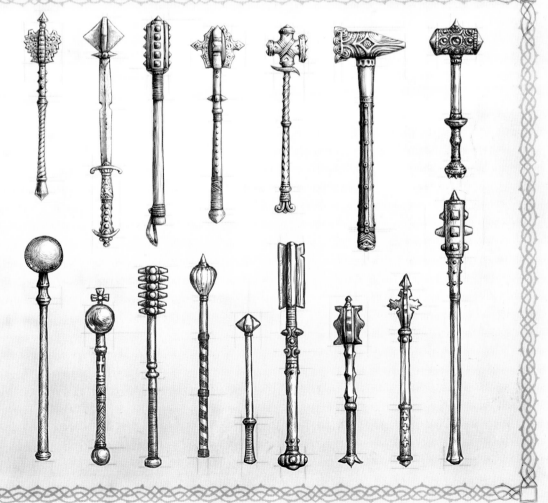

Since the time of the ancients, the shaman and the wise woman have studied and built a special body of lore. These folk of the old ways have a deep understanding of the subtle forces of the moon, the sea, and the flux of the seasons, giving them an uncanny ability to craft healing potions from the botanical world.

As soothsayers, these people know how to penetrate the veil between the seen and the unseen. As healers, they protect and preserve life and the knowledge of life. They cultivate allies in the forest and the field, caring for, and harvesting from, certain trees, plants, and mushrooms, as a shepherd would his sheep.

The forest-dwelling healers who study the arcana of plant lore are perhaps best symbolized by the boline, that moon-bladed knife so well suited for the harvesting of plants.

THE ANTIQUE
BOLINE OF A
WISE WOMAN

After the boline is used to gather the required herbs, mushrooms, vines, and other exotic ingredients, a healer uses spells and secret recipes to combine them into salves, unctions, potions, and teas.

THE SONG OF THE FOREST

Chant and song play an important role in the life of a healer. Music alone can work magic when used in the right way, and when it is combined with plant lore, the healer's art is greatly magnified. Spells can be cast forth upon the wind, and ancient secrets can be coaxed from flowers, vines, and trees.

A FOREST-DWELLING HEALER

CHAPTER 5 — ROGUES & THIEVES

One of the most secretive groups operating within the territories of New Perigord is the Thieves' Guild. This mysterious society operates in the shadows, meeting only in the hidden chambers and tunnels beneath the cobbled streets, or in disguise. Its code is of silence and stealth, and its members even communicate with a secret cryptolect known as the "Rogues' Cant." This language lets them speak with layered meanings, to keep their fellowship safe from penetration and discovery.

Despite their covert training and evasive ways, some members are trusted agents of the emperor himself.

In the distant past, when the first Shining Emperor raised a great host and rode down the wicked slave masters from the ebon Tower of Seryu, it was the Thieves' Guild that saved his noble effort. The filthy minions of enslavement had infiltrated almost every palace and castle in the land, and without the aid of the roguish ones, the slave masters would not have been routed out.

To this day, a dark power emanates from that stinking Tower of Seryu, and the Thieves' Guild is ever vigilant of its reach and influence. The assassins of Galliene work to slay and impoverish any upstart whose lusts embrace the old and evil ways. When nefarious cults and malicious fraternities arise from the dust of the past, it is the rogues who are the eyes and ears in the night. The emperor knows well that the best way to fight shadows is with shadows.

When foreign slavers come with ships to prey upon the folk of New Perigord, or when weak-willed nobles succumb to the demonic influence of greed or cruelty, they can expect to find a moonlit blade at their throats. It may not happen right away, but it will happen. The agile agents of the Thieves' Guild remember the past that others would rather forget, and with feline grace, they move vigilantly against the serpentine creep of evil.

Of note is the fact that rogues are often beloved by the masses, despite the lawlessness and obscurity of their guild, for when they crack the coffers of corruption, they always disperse some of the ill-gotten gold to the poor and the disenfranchised.

The pommel is designed for sliding on a spider-silk zip line.

The cross emblem of a sea rogue

NICKNAME:
Moonsilk

The small "moon" button can lock or unlock the sword in its scabbard.

HERE ARE TWO FINE EXAMPLES OF LIGHT AND DEADLY SWORDS, CUSTOM MADE FOR THE SHADOWMAIDENS OF GALLIENE CITY.

POISON BUTTON

NICKNAME:
Saltwound

POISON NICHE

Tiny nautical instruments are built into the guard.

The entire sword is made of rust-resistant metals.

The spiked hand guard is ideal for brawling while boarding a ship.

Venom can be applied to the blade by pushing the larger "moon" button while the sword is drawn from the scabbard.

A small compass is located in the pommel.

By land or sea, rogues and thieves ply their stealthy trade.

The rogues of Galliene sail the fastest ballista ships in the Northern Hemisphere. Their specialized harpoons can tether and leash an enemy ship for boarding or slash through the rigging and sails of pursuers. The rogues are also sanctioned by the emperor to attack and plunder the ships of enemy nations.

The Thieves' Guild prides itself on the art of infiltration, and thus it cultivates a particular expertise in acrobatics, climbing, rappelling, and the use of spider-silk zip lines. Master thieves can get past defenses that would otherwise thwart the siege attempts of entire armies.

The kind of spider silk that is employed for zip lines is very rare and extremely difficult to acquire, as it comes from the giant rock spiders that inhabit the steaming jungles near the waistline of the world. Special bows and crossbows are used to shoot and affix the silk from afar so that a thief can slide along the web as quiet as a twilight breeze.

And what works for infiltration also works for exfiltration and escape. The rogues can hit and run and be gone like flitting shadows — away on their silken lines, beyond capture.

A shadowmaiden from Galliene whisks along a zip line toward the tower of her chosen mark: a baron known to be plotting against the Archon of Galliene.

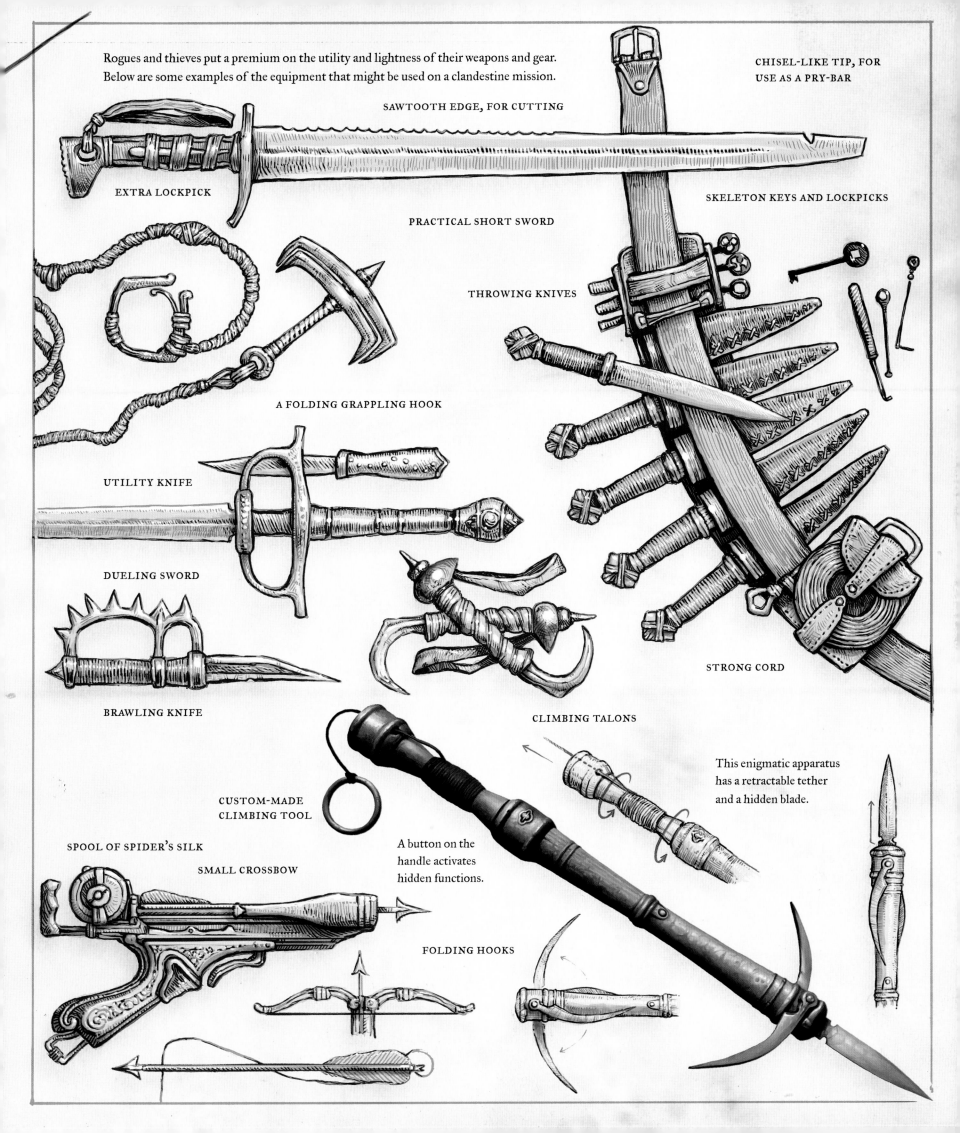

Rogues and thieves put a premium on the utility and lightness of their weapons and gear. Below are some examples of the equipment that might be used on a clandestine mission.

CHISEL-LIKE TIP, FOR USE AS A PRY-BAR

SAWTOOTH EDGE, FOR CUTTING

EXTRA LOCKPICK

PRACTICAL SHORT SWORD

SKELETON KEYS AND LOCKPICKS

THROWING KNIVES

A FOLDING GRAPPLING HOOK

UTILITY KNIFE

DUELING SWORD

BRAWLING KNIFE

CLIMBING TALONS

STRONG CORD

CUSTOM-MADE CLIMBING TOOL

This enigmatic apparatus has a retractable tether and a hidden blade.

SPOOL OF SPIDER'S SILK

SMALL CROSSBOW

A button on the handle activates hidden functions.

FOLDING HOOKS

A TEAM OF ROGUES LIGHTENING THE
COFFERS OF AN OPPRESSIVE BARON

PART II

ON TRAVEL BEYOND THE FIELDS OF MAN, AND
THE PRESENCE OF NON-HUMAN SOCIETIES

THE GREEN PERIGORD

The Green Perigord is a wild and mysterious place full of the strange, fey magic of fairy folk. The climate is cool. Year-round mists predominate, and the dripping forests are dense enough to be lost in forever. Many who wander into them are never seen again. Those who live to describe their travels in this place talk of changing features and disappearing trails. Brooks, springs, and mountain cataracts can appear or disappear in a day's time. The exact lay of the land does not look the same from month to month, and the old-growth trees are said to creep around when no one is looking.

The elves that live here socialize with humans on occasion; however, do not expect the same interactions with all fairies — some are shy, while others are actually hostile. Certain people, when showing proper respect for the region, can travel unhindered, but others are not so lucky. Be careful, and take this advice: Don't even think of going to the Eldritch Isle; it is simply too dangerous.

THE RED PERIGORD

The Red Perigord is a region of rolling hills, mineral-rich mountains, and grassy, open steppes. It is also home to the dwarven people, who burrow into the rocky mountainside for ore, gems, and also security. Most dwarves are friendly to humans, but it is proper to announce neutral intention if passing anywhere near the Dwarven Mines. These sturdy folk are very anxious about trespassers near their vaults. The common protocol is to climb a hill and then glint sunlight upon bright steel, reflecting the light back and forth across the crags and peaks. Do this patiently, and a dwarven scout will signal back in a similar fashion, indicating that you are invited to travel onward. If you stay put and continue signaling, you are asking for contact, and you will soon be met by an entourage of dwarves — if they care to meet you.

The Meadowlands

Nestled in the valleys between the Green and the Red Perigords is a patchwork of human settlement known as the Meadowlands. It is a bountiful frontier with lush and fertile earth, though the residents must barricade themselves cautiously behind stone walls and gated villas. It is also a very independent place, on the outermost fringe of the empire, and the self-reliant folk here would have it no other way.

Extending eastward out of the Meadowlands is the old trading road, now seldom trodden. The ruins of Thistletop Castle loom large over the quiet flagstones of this byway as a reminder of glorious days when the beacons of Gray Oak flared at the slightest stirring of trouble. Now the moss-covered walls and weather-beaten towers sit darkly mute and abandoned.

To the north of the lonely road, in the shadow of the Silvernail Mountains, are the hills and dales where civilization was born. This massive swale is full of ancient shrines, broken-down basilicas, and the bone-white columns of mighty elder pantheons. No one even remembers the gods for whom these sacraria were built. Screeching griffins nest in the worn edifices of marble, and centaur herds run wild through the fallow fields and dry moats. Satyrs and fauns play their solemn and breathy tunes through the thighbones of forgotten kings, and humans are rarely seen.

When dauntless adventurers do come to this historic place, they seek the hoards, relics, and treasures that lie in the countless hiding places, caves, and overgrown monuments that dot the landscape. These adventurers must of course brave the beasts, monsters, and prehistoric guardians that slumber in this antique landscape. Do not be rash or incautious, as there are dangers in the Borderlands better left sleeping.

The only remaining holdout of civilization in this primordial place of volcanoes and desolate heather is that of the Minotaur race. The great herds still dwell unperturbed by the ravages of time in their megalithic stone cities and mazes. They are impassive and neutral, staying out of almost all the conflicts that boil within the Perigords. Not even the smoking destroyer, that tall promontory known as the Mountain of Ash, can displace them: The herds know by deep instinct when the volcanic eruptions will come, and they retreat to their walled alcoves and deep undercities, avoiding the poisonous blasts and fiery winds of the mountain. When the inky clouds part and the ashes disperse, the Minotaurs stoically tread back out to their apiaries and fields of clover to resume their normal lives.

If you travel this far and wish to be greeted by the Minotaurs, to engage their hospitalities or use their shelters, it is customary to bring them gifts of fine axes, which are among their favorite of all things. No other gift will better open their insular world to you for exploration, unless you can come by some rare elfin honey, which they also love.

The Borderlands

CHAPTER 6 — ELVES & FAIRIES

The kingdom of the fairies is concealed within the sheltering forests of the Green Perigord region. The curious magic of this numinous place defies description: one must see firsthand the pale azure mountains and aquamarine fields to appreciate its astonishing beauty. It is strangely alive, this otherworld inhabited by a wide range of fairy folk.

A partial list of the denizens of the Green Perigord includes the elusive wee folk, gnomes, sylphs, undines, tree maidens, and various nature spirits that are fleetingly glimpsed by the alert traveler. Such a list should also include the arboreal folk known as the High Elves, the most humanlike beings in the green realm of the wood and the field, and the most social of all the fairies.

Though the High Elves are the most reliably tolerant and friendly of all the fairies, they do not suffer fools or the hostile trespasses of the unwelcome into their sacred groves. When trouble comes to their forest, they are the staunchest defenders of their home.

High Elves have very keen eyesight and are unmatched with bow and arrow; they protect vast territories and can strike at great range.

To further confound invaders, the elves set traps and enchantments, including spike-laden pits and barriers of thornbush and carnivorous vine. Stalwart intruders, if they manage to penetrate the guarded thickets, will face the withering fire of close-range javelins and the singing steel blades of elfin swords.

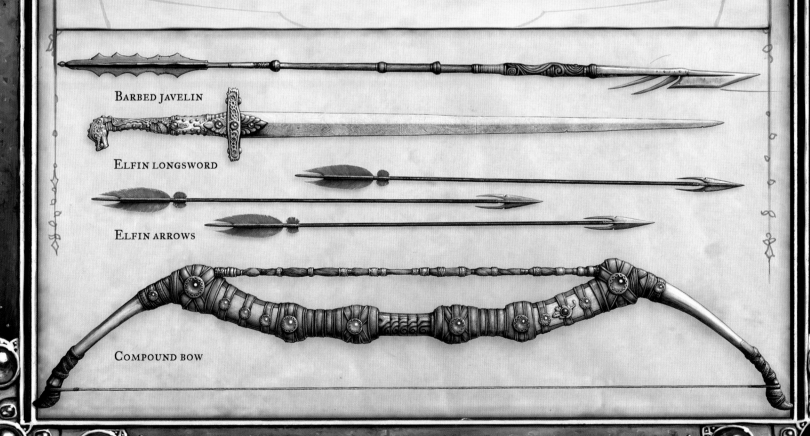

BARBED JAVELIN

ELFIN LONGSWORD

ELFIN ARROWS

COMPOUND BOW

COMMONLY ENCOUNTERED SPIRITS

Most experienced travelers in the uplands, waterways, and strands of the Green Perigord describe vivid sightings of nature spirits. These descriptions usually focus on an enthralling beauty. But be heedful of danger should you see them, and remember that beauty and kindness do not always go hand in hand.

TREE MAIDENS

These graceful nymphs are so sweet that they can steal your heart. Yet they have no mercy or love, and they might lull you to an endless sleep.

WILL-O'-THE-WISPS

These glowing sylphs will often appear in the moorlands, especially near burbling brooks and artesian springs. They retreat alluringly when approached, thereby leading many curious souls astray upon the mires.

MERROWS AND UNDINES

These water spirits call out to passing ships with melancholy songs. Many weak-willed sailors have been destroyed by drifting into reefs and rocks while trying to reach the beautiful mermaids who sing and wave.

These creatures can cast a spell upon you, and it is best to stuff your ears with wax and lash the rudder in a safe position rather than succumb to the heartless magic of the mermaids.

If you attempt to make contact with nature spirits, do so with all caution.

The warnings presented here should not imply that all nature spirits are malicious — they often do harm without meaning any at all. Their lack of compassion is due to the dearth of what humans call a "soul."

It is rumored that humans can develop an affinity with the fey ones and even immunity to the pitfalls and perils of contact with them. Some old tales insinuate that friendship and love can develop. It is whispered that an elemental spirit can thus attain its own soul in the process of finding genuine human love.

ADVENTURING IN THE GREEN PERIGORD

Exploring the shimmering forests and hair-raising terrain of the fairylands can be a very rewarding experience. If you are genteel and approach the woods with the proper reverence, the Green Perigord might open its paths to you, presenting an unmatched avenue for adventure and gain. There are caches of treasure, gold, and jewels; ancient tablets inscribed with secrets; and hidden arsenals of magic weapons to be found.

SOME NOTABLE FEATURES OF THE GREEN PERIGORD LANDSCAPE

Bogs: Marshy turf; treacherous to cross.

Mushroom rings: Places of fey magic where small fairies gather.

Fairy mounds and dolmens: Ancient tombs made of earth and rock.

Monoliths: Gigantic standing stones that mark the ley lines of energy.

Passage tombs: Huge fortresslike tombs where elfin kings are buried.

Cairn stones: Mysterious mounds and piles of rock.

Sacred groves: The stands of trees where High Elves dwell.

COMMON FAIRY FOLK

SOCIABLE FAIRIES: These are usually lighthearted and friendly creatures.

Sheoques: Small pixies and sprites that live among the peat bogs and thorn hedges.

Gnomes: A kind of wee folk that live in little earthen houses or near toadstools.

LONESOME FAIRIES: This class of creature dwells alone and may be neutral or unfriendly, depending on the situation.

Banshee: A howling spirit that will haunt the area where life has been recently lost.

Starved man: Thin and pale; known to appear suddenly, begging for food. Feed it to avoid its agitated curses.

ANTISOCIAL FAIRIES: These fairies tend to cause mischief if disturbed.

Barrow men: Strange fairy folk that dwell in dolmens and passage tombs.

Firbolg: An ancient race of wee folk that are shy and withdrawn. They become thoroughly grouchy if bothered.

Headless: Spooky and hostile wanderers of the dark forests.

An elfin marksman prepares to shoot the distinctive arrows of his royal household at an approaching threat. One can identify the elfin house by the shape of the arrowheads.

Royal archers are trained in the arts of reconnaissance and woodland camouflage.

HIGH ELVES

High Elves are the tall and pale natives of the Green Perigord. They live in resplendent chateaus built amid the boughs of sturdy old trees. These elves divide their turf into kingdoms, with royal houses to rule each stretch of forest. A royal house considers its personal territory to be a sacred grove and sovereign land.

It is nearly impossible to find these tree dwellings, unless you are a welcomed guest. Otherwise, the paths you attempt to travel will not lead to the tree manses at all. If you do somehow stumble near the actual location of a sacred grove, enchantments will hide the buildings and their glowing, cheerful windows from view.

If you are unwelcome to the grove, the guards will make their presence known by firing warning shots with their trademark red arrows.

ROYAL ELFIN MARKSMEN

A marksman of an elfin royal house can move among the treetops as swiftly as a giant spider and with the stealth of a praying mantis. These elite archers use the compound bow as well as a highly accurate and very compact shortbow to fire rapid volleys of arrows. Their light hair blends with the dappled sunlight upon the surrounding foliage, and their green cloaks blend with the mossy boles of the trees. Their one reckless indiscretion is the bright red dye that is used to color their deadly arrows.

THE COMPACT SHORTBOW OF AN ELITE ELFIN ARCHER

AN ELFIN TREE DWELLING

CHAPTER 7 DWARVES

Dwarven culture thrives in the Red Perigord, especially near the rich deposits of the lofty Ironbelt Mountains. For security, the dwarves burrow deep into the solid rock. They mostly keep to their own kind, hoping to mine, smelt, and craft in peace, and they will mount a vigorous defense against unwelcome intruders. The old sagas tell us that dwarves cooperate with humankind and elves, at least during epic times of war. But for the most part, they hold all other cultures at a neutral distance. They will make exception for peaceful delegations and traders, and it is common knowledge that they will pay a nice bounty for the ears of a hobgoblin.

CULLBRINGER

SKULLFIST

DWARVEN ANCESTRAL WEAPONS

The dwarven scout here is depicted with hastily made weapons, crafted from melted-down mining tools, a common practice when the dwarven tribes must match an invading threat. The highest-ranking warriors, on the other hand, keep weapons of the very finest sort. The most precious of these are the ancestral swords and axes from the ancient-most of days, when dwarves swept out of the mountains like wolfhounds — into the fray of the great wars.

KING-BREAKER

ORE-KEEPER

BELLARION

THE TOOTH OF BRANNOR

A DWARVEN MINE ENTRANCE ...

CAMOUFLAGED BY MOSS

DWARVEN TOOLS AND OTHER MISCELLANY

Many dwarven mining implements, such as the maul (left), hammer (above), and pick (below), serve as utilitarian tools in peaceful times or as weapons during an encounter or conflict.

ABOVE: A coin pouch, for keeping gold, silver, gems, and other treasures, next to a small tinderbox, which holds a flint and steel for fire starting

Dwarven jewelers, lapidaries, and engravers are famous throughout New Perigord for making lovely and ornate rings, necklaces, and other items, such as the brooch to the left.

BELOW LEFT: The tribal knife of a dwarven artificer, with a sheath that holds additional tools for the working of leather, along with a file for keeping steel blades in good repair

A small hatchet for woodcrafting and various delicate hammering tasks

A small repair hammer for extra-fine metalwork

Long, long ago, when dwarves first colonized the Ironbelt Mountains, they built cheerful hamlets and villages and lived in the open air. Now only a few of those surface dwellings remain, and the rest are windswept ruins. Hobgoblins from the horrible Frostmarch have taken over, despite a fierce and ongoing struggle with the fairy folk of the northern forests. The human barricades and ramparts in the Meadowlands have done little to stop the vulturine assaults of the goblin marauders.

Thus have the hardy dwarves dug like badgers, building mountain palisades and underground citadels to take their cover from the rapacious raiders. It is just as well, because the ancient Necropolis to the east has since erupted with plagues of undead, and fell creatures have lately thronged forth from the murky waters of the Black Fens and the polluted Acid Basin.

Many dwarven kings brood in their mountain vaults, dreaming of a new day when they can retake the open fields and sun-drenched mountainsides by force. Others turn their minds only to gems and gold, content to burrow ever deeper into the dark bowels of the earth.

By the light of a glowing brazier, a king of the dwarves drinks a horn of spiced grog while ruminating about his underground realm.

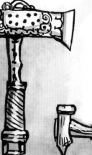

SIDE VIEW OF A DWARVEN MINE ENTRANCE

A dwarven fortress vault, built deep into the protective mountain rock. Dwarves have elaborate defenses to keep out thieves, giant snakes, and the nasty, dreaded hobgoblins — who continually lust for dwarven treasure, slaves, and steel.

Deeper in the mines, the dwarves jealously guard treasure vaults, dormitories, armories, crafting centers, cisterns, dark lakes, and gigantic excavated halls.

VIEW PORTS

FINAL GATE TO THE DWARVEN UNDERWORLD

MAIN ENTRANCE

TRAPDOOR WITH NET

ROTATING FLOOR THAT TURNS INTO SIEGE BARRIER

DRAWBRIDGE

These dire defenses allow the dwarves to send any raiding hobgoblins hooting and hollering in retreat.

Though dwarves also spend time aboveground, they retreat to the safety of their vaulted mines in times of trouble.

Dwarves are experts at mechanical engineering, and they know how to power all manner of devices with clever use of weights and counterweights.

Dwarves use torches, lamps, braziers, and candles to fend off the darkness, but they also cultivate luminous fungus, which casts an incredible glow.

By living on readily available mushrooms, blind fish from underground rivers, and giant cave crabs, dwarves can withstand nearly any length of siege.

DWARVEN CROSSBOW WITH A VARIETY OF QUARRELS

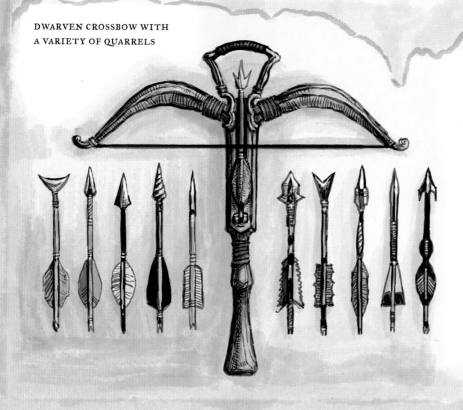

SUBTERRESTRIAL CONFLICT

The compact stature of the dwarven people lends itself to life underground. By the same token, these stout warriors can fight in the tight confines of their tunnels and passageways like angry wolverines. They are adept at building subsurface bulwarks and defenses along with traps that can deplete entire battalions of a hobgoblin army.

While dwarves are experts at close-quarters battle, they do not neglect the use of ranged attacks. Their stocky crossbows will blast armor-piercing bolts into the midst of an intruding force.

THE PERSONAL EFFECTS OF
A DWARVEN VAULT MINER

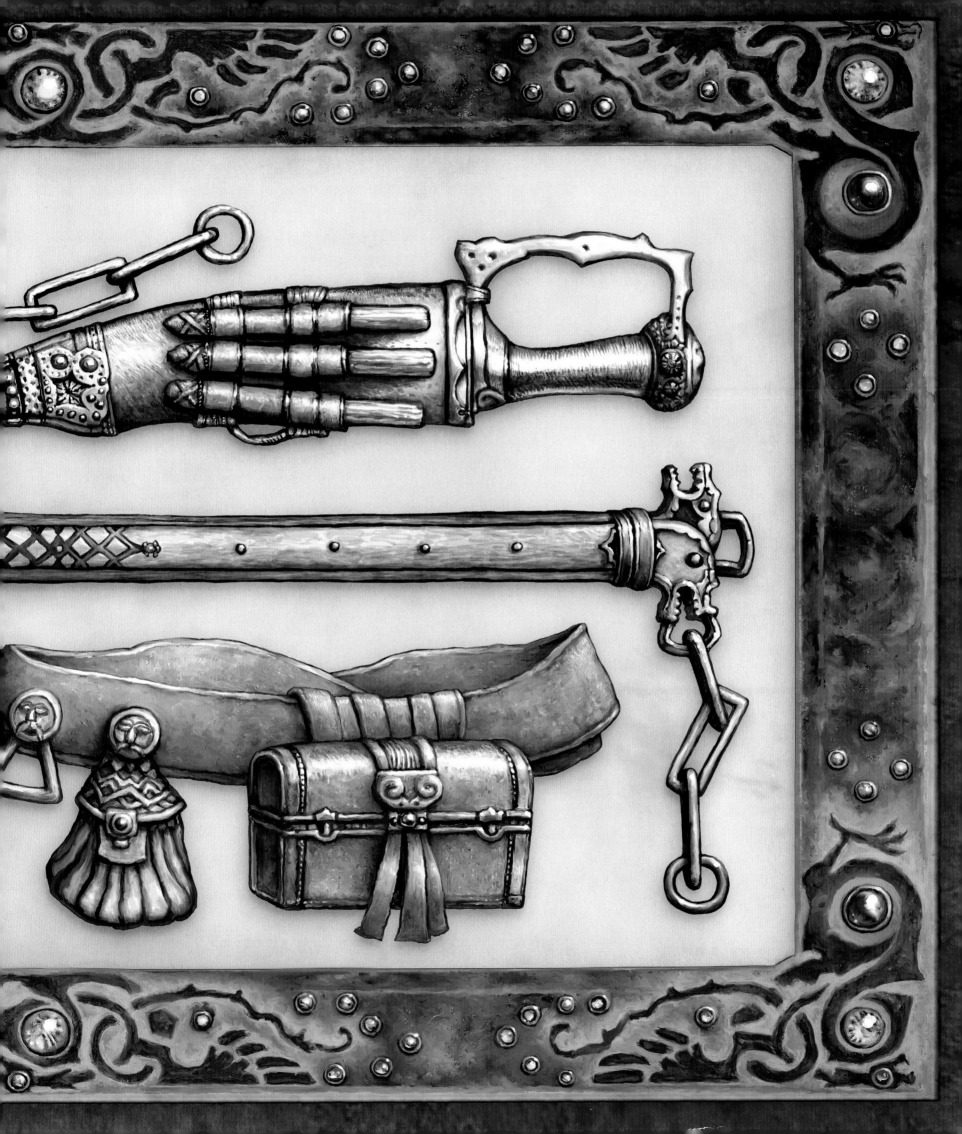

CHAPTER 8 MINOTAURS

In the immense valleys of the Borderlands, betwixt the arboreal civilization of the elves and the mountainous presence of the hobgoblins, one finds the indomitable Minotaur race. They live in megalithic cities: maze-like stone fortifications built when the earth was young, when a forgotten elder race ruled the land. The oldest parchments say that the Minotaurs were the prized guardians of the ancient city-states and terraced hilltops. Yet now the temples, plazas, and aqueducts are all but ruined, mere skeletons of marble and graven stone, faded like distant memories. But in the time-worn fastness of their labyrinths, the hardy Minotaur herds remain and thrive.

Minotaur Axes

The paintings on the walls of excavated ruins in the Borderlands show a priest class of people who kept an alliance with the Minotaur herds by presenting them with axes as gifts. More obscure paintings also hint at less friendly herds — fierce and carnivorous — that were kept and fed by the sacrificial offerings of wicked priesthoods. The legends portray the dark herds as rising up and becoming the destroyers of the temples they were bribed to guard.

Most herds of the modern era are plant eaters and peaceable enough. Travelers occasionally report certain alarming encounters, though, apparently with the wicked remnants of the man-eating Minotaurs of old. These creatures are almost always found near temple ruins of blackest stone, so be leery of such sinister places.

For the most part, the Minotaur race is very civilized, and as long as you don't cross them, they will respect you.

Not all Minotaurs appear alike, and in fact they can be quite varied in appearance.

Despite their differences, Minotaurs get along well.

Minotaurs have some affinity for elves, and they trade certain goods with them on a regular basis. However, they hate hobgoblins and have never been in a state of peace with them. Humans have a fairly neutral relationship with the herds.

Minotaurs are related distantly to centaurs and fauns, but they do not always get along with them. When these creatures fight, it is mostly without weapons, in a display of strength and dominance that can still be stunningly brutal.

Minotaurs group together into families, and the families group by the thousands to form a herd.

Minotaurs fight as herd animals, using the subtle instincts of group intelligence to augment their abilities. Just as a school of fish or a flight of sparrows can twist and turn with instantaneous grace, the herd can fight with unified intent and collective awareness. Thus the herd battles like a beast with a thousand axes.

This expertise in battle has preserved the Minotaur herds through eons of invasion and turmoil in their historic corner of the Green Perigord. Though battles have raged around them, they rarely give up an inch of territory.

The map below shows the general territory of the Minotaur people.

GREEN PERIGORD

MINOTAUR HERDS

THE BORDERLANDS

THE MEADOWLANDS

BLACK PERIGORD

THE EASTERN PROVINCES

GRAY PERIGORD

RED PERIGORD

Most Minotaur labyrinths surround ancient temple ruins. The temples are prominent upon hills, and the hills are riddled with tunnels and alcoves. Deeper yet beneath the mountain, down a megalithic flight of stairs, one will usually find an undercity.

The undercity is an entirely self-sufficient Minotaur dwelling, kept secure within the rocky embrace of the earth. Typically, an undercity is maintained by a small resident population, while the main herd lives aboveground. When a threat comes to the labyrinth, the herd retreats to the safety of the undercity.

Only very rarely has an invasion penetrated deep within the undercity of the Minotaurs. There is an entire maze belowground as well that is meant to confound and confuse the uninitiated.

THE AX OF CRONUS

Two examples of axes that were gifted to the herds while the stone temples of the North were yet young

THE AX OF ASPHODEL

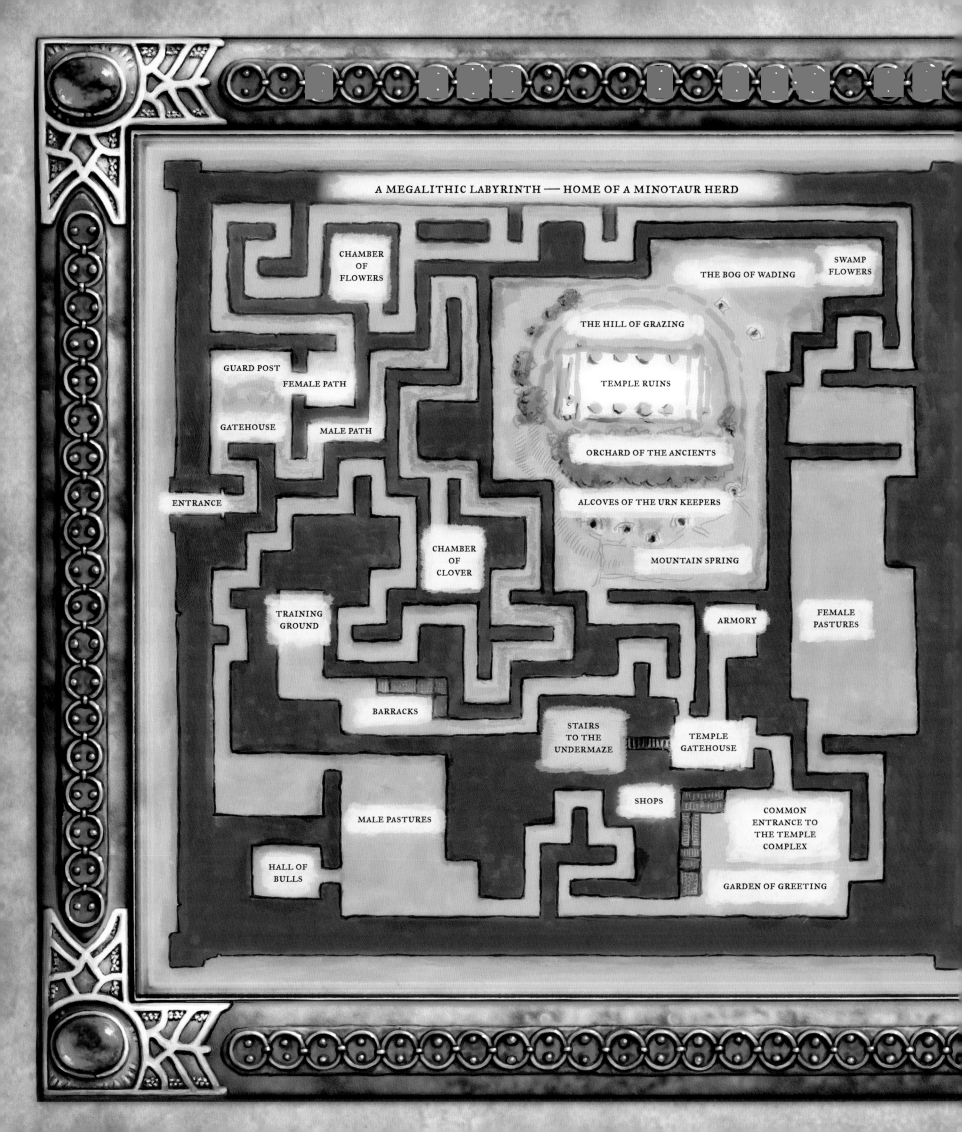

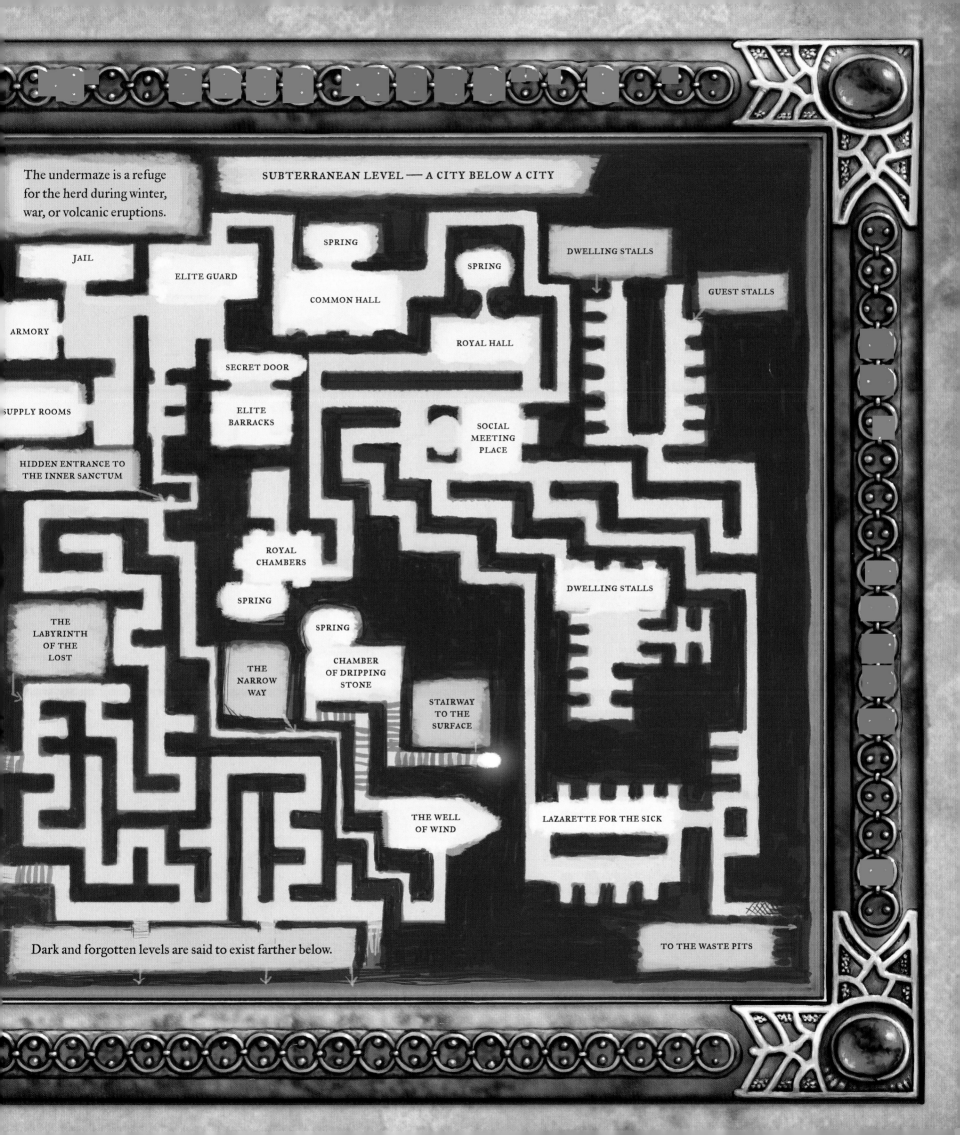

The undermaze is a refuge for the herd during winter, war, or volcanic eruptions.

SUBTERRANEAN LEVEL — A CITY BELOW A CITY

JAIL

ELITE GUARD

SPRING

COMMON HALL

SPRING

DWELLING STALLS

GUEST STALLS

ARMORY

ROYAL HALL

SECRET DOOR

SUPPLY ROOMS

ELITE BARRACKS

SOCIAL MEETING PLACE

HIDDEN ENTRANCE TO THE INNER SANCTUM

ROYAL CHAMBERS

DWELLING STALLS

SPRING

THE LABYRINTH OF THE LOST

SPRING

THE NARROW WAY

CHAMBER OF DRIPPING STONE

STAIRWAY TO THE SURFACE

THE WELL OF WIND

LAZARETTE FOR THE SICK

Dark and forgotten levels are said to exist farther below.

TO THE WASTE PITS

PART III
ON THE DANGERS OF THE BLACK PERIGORD AND ITS VAST TRACTS OF WASTELAND AND WILDERNESS

The region known as the Black Perigord encompasses a huge swath of territory as well as some of the direst threats one can imagine. Travel to this region only if armed, and preferably with an able party.

An increasingly common peril here is the monster we call the hobgoblin. Many large clans of these belligerent brutes have moved down from the North of late.

THE MOUNTAIN OF ASH

The Silvernail Mountains are positively overrun with nasty hobgoblins, especially southeast of the Mountain of Ash.

THE NECROPOLIS

In the ashen midlands below the sweeping infestation of the hobgoblins, one finds the city of the dead — that great and archaic Necropolis. It was built before the time of the first emperor and was once a shining marble monument. Now it is a fetid place, full of horrible necromantic liches and undead horrors.

Nearby, the obsidian-hued Tower Dungeon of Seryu presides over the stench of the region — a reminder of darker days.

The Moridaunt and Marrowdirge rivers bubble out of the crypts and catacombs of the Necropolis like two iodine-colored snakes. They wend into the polluted muck known as the Black Fens, and then farther south to the stunted wastes of the Acid Basin.

These marshy badlands are full of slithering serpents; giant rats; bloated, carrion-eating fish; and innumerable plague-ravaged monsters.

Fell creatures proliferate in the murk and the gloom, making this an especially treacherous place to traverse. Most travelers come here only to pass through to the southern jungle villages or to the cities of the distant and exotic East.

THE BLACK FENS AND THE ACID BASIN

THE KALISATRA MOUNTAINS

The destination of many bold expeditions, this rugged area is teeming with dangerous creatures such as basilisks, wyverns, and other dragons. These terrifying monsters hoard treasure, stashed and added to over the ages, which keeps adventurers coming, despite the tremendous risk. I recommend steering clear of this range until you possess expertise in travel and combat.

THE FROZEN NORTH

The Waste is a grand stretch of cold, desolate land, stalked by giants and gargantuan creatures. There are barbarian towns here and there that have adapted to the harsh climate and treacherous conditions, but it is a sparsely populated place, and for good reason. The warring giants keep all but the bravest souls away.

Tundra fades into purest ice in the glacial North, which is the territory of the biggest of all giants — the Frost Giants. The few who live and travel here do so by virtue of hard-won alliances with the local Frost Giants, or with particular stealth and care. . . . Angry giants are nearly unstoppable, except by powerful siege machinery, special poisons, or high magic.

THE WILD LANDS BEYOND

If you follow the jagged peaks of the Kalisatra Mountain range, they eventually taper off to the Southeast, blending into immense jungles and steaming rain forests. This is a mysterious place that time has nearly forgotten, where huge saurian monsters hunt and graze in uncharted valleys and ancient human tribes live in remote isolation. Even stranger places lie beyond, such as the blackened mountains and stygian wastes of the Burned Land, or the high deserts, where sandships sail across the Sea of Dust. Far-flung civilizations exist beyond these wide deserts and wastelands, but the trip is long and dangerous. Only the best-guarded caravans or the most intrepid parties attempt the journey.

CHAPTER 9 — HOBGOBLINS

Hobgoblins are a larger and stronger variant of the common goblin. They inhabit the high passes and wild mountains where humankind rarely dares to wander. Hobgoblins play different roles in their society, depending on their size and intelligence, but all are trained for the bloodlust of war. Some toil as beasts of burden, sentries, scouts, and soldiers, but the greatest and most fearsome of them become the champions of the clan. When hobgoblins mount a raid or an invasion, they seem to embody the very force of destruction itself.

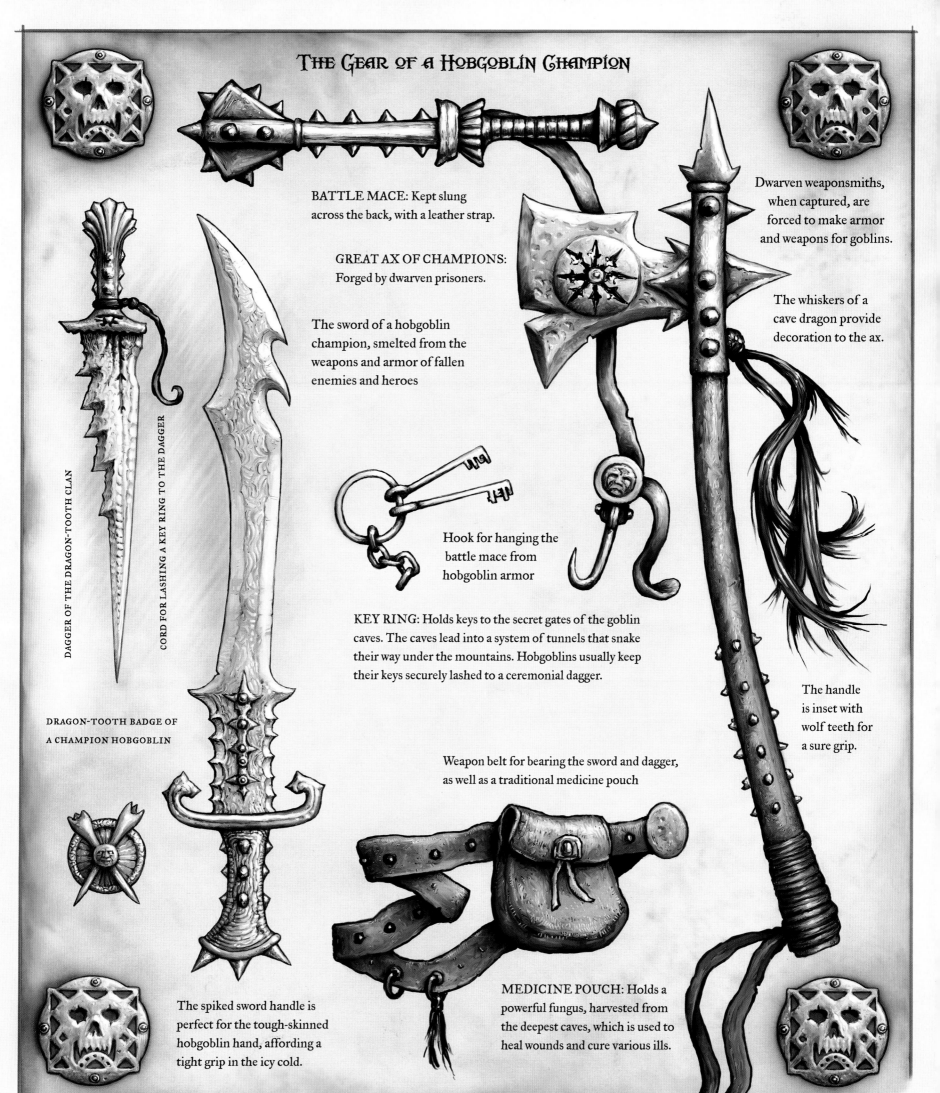

THE GEAR OF A HOBGOBLIN CHAMPION

BATTLE MACE: Kept slung across the back, with a leather strap.

GREAT AX OF CHAMPIONS: Forged by dwarven prisoners.

The sword of a hobgoblin champion, smelted from the weapons and armor of fallen enemies and heroes

Dwarven weaponsmiths, when captured, are forced to make armor and weapons for goblins.

The whiskers of a cave dragon provide decoration to the ax.

DAGGER OF THE DRAGON-TOOTH CLAN

CORD FOR LASHING A KEY RING TO THE DAGGER

Hook for hanging the battle mace from hobgoblin armor

KEY RING: Holds keys to the secret gates of the goblin caves. The caves lead into a system of tunnels that snake their way under the mountains. Hobgoblins usually keep their keys securely lashed to a ceremonial dagger.

The handle is inset with wolf teeth for a sure grip.

DRAGON-TOOTH BADGE OF A CHAMPION HOBGOBLIN

Weapon belt for bearing the sword and dagger, as well as a traditional medicine pouch

The spiked sword handle is perfect for the tough-skinned hobgoblin hand, affording a tight grip in the icy cold.

MEDICINE POUCH: Holds a powerful fungus, harvested from the deepest caves, which is used to heal wounds and cure various ills.

PACK HOBGOBLINS: Like beasts of burden, these slow-witted ones perform the backbreaking labor of portering supplies and digging tunnels. They are often ridden by the lesser goblins, but they tolerate such a thing only if they are kept well fed; otherwise they run amok.

HOBGOBLIN SCOUTS: These are smaller and more agile than the largest of the hobgoblin fighters but strong and fast enough to be skirmishers near the front lines in battle. They are usually posted around the fringes of a clan's territory to keep watch for potential enemies or prey.

HOBGOBLIN CHAMPIONS: When invaders cause trouble in goblin lands or when the mighty clans assemble for war, these brutes are called forth from their deep caverns to rampage and cause terror. Each champion will have a horde of soldiers and servants at his command.

COMMON GOBLINS: These diminutive members of the clan are numerous and dangerous enough in groups, but they are skittish when they are not backed up by their larger kin. Though smaller than true hobgoblins, they do the majority of the hunting of meat.

HOBGOBLIN SOLDIERS: These are mid-ranked creatures in the social order of the goblin clans and form the bulk of their fighting force. These soldiers are inclined to rove in sizable bands beyond their mountain redoubts, raiding and looting those neighbors who cannot mount a sturdy enough defense.

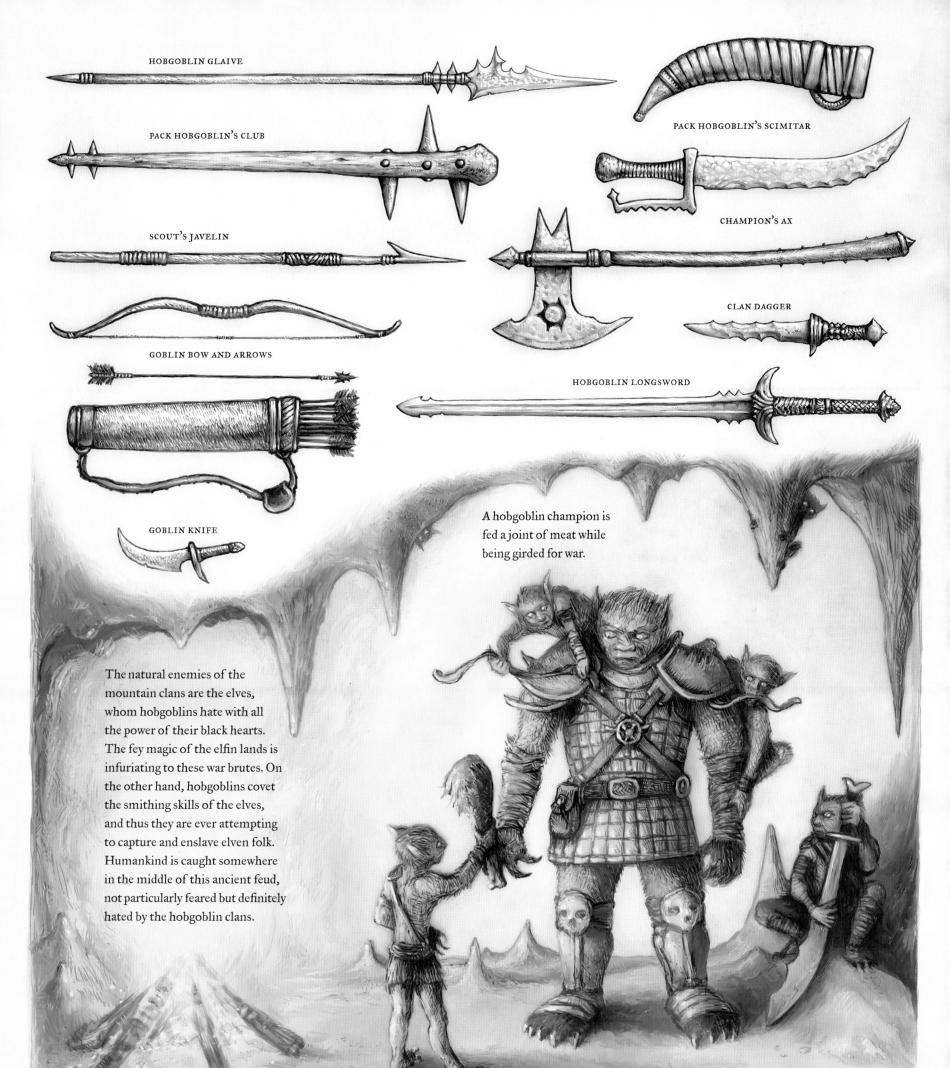

HOBGOBLIN GLAIVE

PACK HOBGOBLIN'S CLUB

PACK HOBGOBLIN'S SCIMITAR

SCOUT'S JAVELIN

CHAMPION'S AX

GOBLIN BOW AND ARROWS

CLAN DAGGER

HOBGOBLIN LONGSWORD

GOBLIN KNIFE

A hobgoblin champion is fed a joint of meat while being girded for war.

The natural enemies of the mountain clans are the elves, whom hobgoblins hate with all the power of their black hearts. The fey magic of the elfin lands is infuriating to these war brutes. On the other hand, hobgoblins covet the smithing skills of the elves, and thus they are ever attempting to capture and enslave elven folk. Humankind is caught somewhere in the middle of this ancient feud, not particularly feared but definitely hated by the hobgoblin clans.

CHAPTER 10

LICHES & UNDEAD

The Necropolis is a loathsome place by day, with weeping stone statuary and bone-strewn pathways. While Sol burns above the horizon, it is almost always deathly quiet: no birds sing but the cackling crows; no dangers openly walk the grounds. The yawning catacombs and musty crypts are another matter, though; they are full of hollow-eyed liches and gruesome undead.

By night, the city of the dead is astir with the macabre. Mists pour over the drab hilltops and into the dilapidated cemeteries, and the sound of crunching bone echoes sharply off the mausoleum walls. Haunted bell towers toll, and pallid ghosts scream startlingly under the cold, starry skies. Do not tarry here after twilight unless you absolutely must!

ABOUT LICHES: Liches are creatures that are sometimes animated for entire ages beyond death. They retain a cruel intelligence in the bloodless marrow of their shriveled remains, and many grow in power over the years. Some are the patient rulers of lost mortuaries or the slimy kings of watery, sunken tombs; others restlessly wander among the leaning gravestones and shrines to stand watch over the ancient boneyards of the Necropolis. When disturbed, these sallow-faced terrors will attack, for they hate any reminder of the living world.

A PARTIAL LIST OF THE DANGEROUS DENIZENS OF THE NECROPOLIS

UNDEAD DANGERS	LIVING DANGERS
Liches	Grave robbers
Skeletons	Necromancers
Zombies	Blood bats
Ghouls	Crypt vipers
Vampires	Carrion wolves
Wights	Savage cannibals
Ghosts	Albino spiders
Wraiths	Man-eating fungus
Mummies	Grotto imps
Gargoyles	Casket worms

WITCH SWORDS: Some of the most powerful liches and undead necromancers wield "witch swords," powerful weapons made with evil relics and thrice-cursed steel. Even the Paladins dread these sable-bladed and darkly radiant swords. The blades are so blighted with the blackest of death-magic that they enable a liche to rule entire armies of undead. The Necropolis is full of these aged swords — along with many other wicked and potent weapons buried during the age of heroes or before.

The shambling liches who come to possess these artifacts wage ghastly war on the world, manifesting their hate by conjuring up mighty hosts of zombies and skeletal warriors.

Less powerful liches who do not yet possess such death-dealing tools seem driven by a madness to gain them: the chaos of these buried weapons calls out to the infernal hearts and greed-infected minds of these emaciated fiends. The evil blades seem to lure, taunt, and beckon through crusty earth and thickest, rust-streaked stone. Thus are the skull-faced wretches of the Necropolis, never at ease, but ever, ever seeking until they should finally claim the baneful objects of their desire.

Some living beings also seek these corrupt witch swords among the charcoal pits of ancient funeral pyres or the unviolated caskets found in countless lost tombs, but this is not a sound idea — the evil magic of these weapons is deplorable.

SKELETONS

These common monsters are reanimated by the dangerous and chaotic magic of necromancy. They do not move and fight by the strength of sinew or muscle but purely by the dark powers of sorcery. Fortunately, they can be defeated by being sufficiently destroyed.

Skeletons especially dislike clerics, perhaps in part due to the bone-smashing maces and clubs that these holy men and women tend to possess.

Liches are expert at casting enchantments upon the bones of the dead to create minions that will be under a powerful thrall. Some skeletons do live with a semblance of their own will, free of the dominant yoke of a controller. This usually occurs when the magic-using master of a skeleton has been destroyed. Many of the smaller bands of undead that assail the living are of this variety. Larger, more organized armies of the undead march under the direction of a master.

ZOMBIES

Most zombies, unless they have become too desiccated or mummified, are bulkier and stronger than mere skeletons. Their grim muscle and flesh also make them more difficult to destroy. That they frequently wear armor doesn't help matters.

The endless catacombs beneath the Necropolis are crawling with countless zombified warriors from eras past. Some guard tombs full of magic items and precious loot, while others gather in the dusky gloom by the conjurations of evil magic to await the order to march to battle.

It seems that, lately, zombie attacks have become more frequent upon the neighboring countryside. Village gossip even claims that the emperor has been moving several legions of Blade Wardens to prepare for a possible zombie invasion. Strange lights have been witnessed around the stygian ruins of Seryu, which is always a bad omen that evil magic is stirring around the Necropolis.

GHOULS

These furtive undead creatures dwell in graveyards and tombs and are drawn to the magic of necromancers and liches like flies to a corpse. Ghouls scuttle around underground by the light of day, usually gnawing on the bones of the dead, but after dusk, they grow more bold and emerge to serve their liche masters. Liches dispatch them to dig and search for weapons and relics so that they might help arm newly summoned skeletons and zombies. Ghouls do have a vicious will of their own, but they still eagerly do the bidding of liches for fear of punishment.

Keep a bright lantern, torch, or magic light at the ready to discourage these hideous scamps from attacking.

Ghouls are somewhat similar to the feral humans of the Acid Basin but are more gray and nocturnal and, most important, undead. They bask in the dark energies of nearby evil and outlive their mortal cousins by ages and ages.

VAMPIRES

During the witching hour of certain nights, as wispy fingers of gray lichen stir in the trees with the dread breath of misty air, evil incantations drone forth from the dark groves of blackened trees, and witches sing eerie songs around twinkling, scattered bonfires. Their calls reverberate beneath the mist and echo between the listing statues of the Necropolis lands. Liches and foul things emerge from hiding and assemble aboveground. On such nights, humankind must be alert, especially in the woods and hilltops. Even the most aloof vampire lords stir on these Sabbath nights — and they don't like to be disturbed.

Unlike the bone-eating ghouls, vampires prefer to feed upon the blood of the living. They rest in sarcophagi in hidden chambers until they rise from their morbid sleep to pursue their depraved nocturnal gatherings and predations. The vampires' eyes shine like pale moons as they keenly seek the drumlike beating of human hearts. The sinister, flashing orbs of hunting vampires can often be spotted among the gargoyle statues and high tower tops of the Necropolis, or they can be seen peering out from the dark doorways of the catacombs below. Do not look straight into the milky, glowing gaze of a vampire for too long, or you might fall under its hypnotic spell!

UNDEAD MINIONS ANSWERING THE SUMMONS OF A LICHE

CHAPTER II

FELL CREATURES

Fell creatures are dangerous animals that are cursed with a rabid and malevolent disease. The disease seems to break out time and time again in the stinking waters of the Black Fens and the eerie wastes of the Acid Basin. Perhaps it is caused by the polluted runoff from the Necropolis, with its legions of buried dead, or perchance from the evil influence emanating out of the filthy Tower Dungeon of Seryu, the evil ruins where chaos-mages once did unspeakable things. However this ill-ness started, the infected creatures come bursting forth unexpectedly, a vicious plague upon the surrounding areas. Some of them manage to travel incredible dis-tances before they are hunted down and eliminated. Others lurk and linger in dark and hidden places, their red, glowing eyes ever searching for prey.

The fell ones are almost countless in their diversity, given that so many species can succumb to the contagious spread of this sickness. It is passed by the bite, sting, or similar wound from an infected vector of this blood-borne foulness.

There are various mammals, reptiles, insects, arachnids, and humanoids that can be afflicted, and all become raving and dire beasts in short order. Thankfully, humans are immune to the revolting distemper of the fell creatures.

"Fell" means inhuman, awful, and cruel; that description matches the frightful syndrome all too well. Even innocuous beasts become a serious threat when they catch this rabid fever.

Fell creatures do not have the wits to use tools, but they possess an arsenal of natural weaponry, combined with a nasty temper.

POISONOUS STINGERS

PINCERS

STICKY WEBS

RABID BITES

HORNS

CLAWS

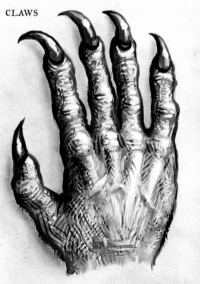

VENOMOUS MANDIBLES

A giant infected scorpion attacks!

It is not certain how this plague arises, but it is known that tainted animals seem to be more common after a certain interval of years.

Wise men have tried to divine from the stars what season may be dangerous or not, but no pattern or prediction can guarantee safety. It is best to be ready to encounter the unexpected at any time.

Even during the quietest years, a seeker might be able to stir up fell creatures from the dark woods or fetid swamps south of the Necropolis. They always seem to lurk there . . . and if you hunt long enough, you will eventually come to know the sight of those terrible red eyes.

For some reason, tiny creatures do not seem to catch the fell disease, but this is not much of a blessing. . . .

Giant monsters such as the marsh scorpion and the hill spider are very readily infected, turning them into terrifying menaces.

Alchemists and sages have pondered the properties of fell creatures' blood for centuries in search of ways to defeat this pestilence. They traditionally use fell blood, with an admixture of other reagents, to make powerful potions and philters.

Certain alchemical potions can be used to enchant weapons, temporarily or permanently, depending on their strength. A weapon enchanted in this way will be more effective against fell creatures, and the beasts are more easily repulsed by properly treated steel.

DEATH-WING

EXAMPLES OF
ENCHANTED SWORDS

DEATH-CLAW

There never seem to be enough hardy and brave souls to act as wardens and protectors of the remote farms and granges, especially when a serious bout of the fell menace strikes. In such times, the folk of the wilder places must flee to gated villas and walled forts for protection.

When this occurs, only a determined effort will cleanse the countryside of evil. If you have a stout heart and a sharp sword, you shall never lack for employment in the vulnerable outlands.

Any lord or baron worth his salt pays a handsome fee for the removal of these ominous creatures, and many daring adventurers make a lifetime career of such hunting.

Giant rats are a common kind of fell creature, probably because they dwell in the swamps and fens in great numbers.

It is advisable never to hunt these rats alone, since they can quickly overwhelm their foe. They are rarely encountered as solitary animals, and where one is found, there is likely to be an entire hostile colony nearby.

Below are some of the bipeds and humanoids that commonly succumb to the fell disease.

FERAL MAN

YEREN

BEAST MAN

TROGLODYTE

A subterranean animal that can see and hunt in absolute darkness, the troglodyte is about half the height of the average human.

A forest and swamp dweller that scours the land with an omnivorous hunger, the beast man is said to smell awful.

Adapted to extreme environments like the Kalisatra Mountains, the yeren has thick white fur.

Rumored to be closely related to humans but sadly devolved into a bestial thing, the feral man is a crafty wretch.

A HUNTER TRACKS DOWN
SOME FELL CREATURES.

CHAPTER 12 OTHER MONSTERS

New Perigord is home to a strange and complicated ecology of creatures we call monsters. Insects and arachnids big enough to trap swamp trolls in their webs routinely prowl the brush, and in the wasteland and the wilds, bizarre and alarmingly large things are everywhere. The landscape is like a gem-colored garden wilderness in some areas, with beautiful saurian creatures that graze peacefully on the treetops. Yet its loveliness is offset by the presence of fierce predators and man-eating plants. Even certain tamer beasts can be dangerous if approached too recklessly.

Some monsters deserve special warning and should be avoided. Griffins, for instance, don't like being fussed with at all. They have even made a habit of using steel weapons to keep people away. Larger threats by far, wyverns, dragons, and hydras stake out swaths of territory that should be treated with the utmost respect. The temptation is always to track down a dragon's nest to pluck treasure from its stashes of shiny things. But dragon nests are also lined with adventurers' bones. Hobgoblins are known to shear a few whiskers off the occasional sleeping cave dragon, but don't let that encourage you — even hobgoblins refuse to provoke the bigger specimens.

The coastlines of New Perigord are stunning to behold, with beaches, coves, and waters teeming with colorful sea life. Yet there are some dangers to be aware of, most especially if you head out to sea. Experienced sailors and fishermen know the methods to avoid attracting too much attention from water monsters, but even fast, careful ships are attacked now and then. Kraken and giant octopi use hideous tentacles to ensnare ships, and sea dragons and water serpents coil around vessels with their slimy, long bodies. There are also giant snapping turtles that cunningly disguise themselves as floating kelp beds: approach them too closely, and they strike with a bite that can splinter the hull of an imperial warship. If you sail into the deeper waters, things become even stranger: Sailors report seeing drifting leviathans staring up from the depths, described as monsters with huge faces and unblinking, incandescent eyes. What these creatures can be is hotly debated in the wharfside taverns worldwide, but it is agreed that they are intelligent and massive.

Moreover, one cannot begin to discuss the dangers of New Perigord without describing the actual giants that live there, ranging in size from the surly ogre [roughly four times the height of a man] all the way to the elder Frost Giants [about twenty times the height of a man]. Usually, Frost Giants wage war only on other giants, but if you catch their attention, it may not bode well. These colossal beings are so powerful, it is said that even the biggest demons from the Lake of Fire fear and avoid them.

Now and then, monster-hunting teams are put together to directly confront and deal with certain large threats, but for the most part, gargantuan creatures of the land and sea are merely avoided. Experienced travelers generally learn to move with appropriate skill to come and go across the map without provoking the likes of dragons and giants.

Dragons

Dragons and their scaly, winged ilk roam throughout the wilderness of New Perigord, but most of them prefer to keep their nests on high mountain crags or in remote caves. The wolf-headed dragon [above] is a common predator near the foothills of the Kalisatra Mountains. It has also been known to nest by the hundreds in the blackened stonework of the massive spire of Seryu. In another age, that tower was once home to a great black dragon, but it is surely gone now, or the much smaller wolf-headed dragons wouldn't be seen near the place. Bigger dragons will eat smaller kin without hesitation.

VARIATIONS OF THE DRAGON
Wyvern: Much like a common dragon, but it has only two legs, instead of four.
Hydra: Has multiple serpentine necks and heads and often lives in swamps and lakes.
Sea dragon: Entirely aquatic, with a long, legless body.

A SIZE COMPARISON OF SOME LAND-DWELLING CREATURES
(each of roughly average height per species)

FROM LEFT TO RIGHT:
Human, elf, dwarf, Minotaur, hobgoblin, griffin, cave dragon, and saurian beast

A SIZE COMPARISON OF SEVERAL LARGE SEA CREATURES
(each of roughly average height per species)

FROM LEFT TO RIGHT:
Small merchant ship, human archer, kraken, sea dragon, giant snapping turtle, and last, a mysterious leviathan

EVASION AT SEA

Moving at speed through deep water will help avoid some attacks, but most sailors also keep big, weighted sacks of meat to toss overboard as distractions and lures if attacked by sea monsters.

TIPS FOR TRAVEL AROUND DRAGONS, GIANTS, AND OTHER LARGE MONSTERS

Look for tracks or claw marks that might indicate that an area is marked territory: if so, take extra precautions.

Most large land predators have vision that is sensitive to movement. If you are very still when under the gaze of a giant beast, you may go unnoticed. Dragons like shiny things, so cover armor or bright gold or silver jewelry with a cloak when passing near a dragon's territory.

There are merchants and vendors in most cities and towns who sell plant oils and formulations of scent known to mask human odor. If you must travel up-wind of a large predator, it is a good idea to disguise your scent.

Frost Giants have been known to have loose alliances with humans, depending on the situation. Some human folk have provided for the giants in some way, and they are thus tolerated on the giants' turf. But the giants often fight among themselves, so humans can easily get caught in the middle of epic battles over territory.

GIGANTIC WEAPONS
Frost Giants carry weapons that are as tall as the grand pines of the North. When these giants rampage and do battle, these colossal weapons can shear the very mountaintops or smite entire swaths of the forest into splintered ruin.

FROST GIANTS
These are the largest of all creatures in the Perigords, much bigger even than the saurian beasts of the misty jungle. They tend to roam the alps and glaciers of the frozen North, hunting mammoths and other suitably large prey.

BELOW: A human skeleton and a common swamp troll are compared in height to the weapons of several different types of giants.

A MOUNTAIN GIANT'S TREE-HILTED BASHING SWORD ——————
The moss-covered behemoths known as Mountain Giants dwell near bigger mountains, but they stay out of the way of Frost Giants if they can help it.

A TITAN'S SLEEK AND SHARP SWORD ——————
Covered with caked-on layers of white clay, the spooky Titans meditate among towering shrines of the distant East.

A HILL GIANT'S BROAD-BLADED WEAPON ——————
The medium-size Hill Giants live in large canyons and caverns amid the area known as the Waste.

A CYCLOPS'S HEAD-LOPPER ——————
The one-eyed brutes called Cyclopes are found on the islands and coastlines of the Lentic Sea.

AN OGRE'S BLUNT YET STOUT KNIFE ——————
Ogres live in caves around the Kalisatra Mountain range.

SWAMP TROLL ——————
Lives in the lower Moridaunt River area.

HUMAN ——————
Six-foot human skeleton

:: Final Note ::

It is here, friend, that I shall take my leave, stepping aside for a time to rest my weary pen. My accounting has been less than complete, and I have surely left out many important details, which you will have to find out for yourself as you delve into the mysteries of this place called New Perigord. I hope you will not blame me for the many gaps in my narrative, since the Perigords are fuller of wonders than could be listed or described in the lifetime of a mere mortal. Yet I also hope my notes and illustrations will serve you well as you pursue your own adventures.

Whether you walk the roads and paths of the Gray Perigord or the untrodden wilderness of the farthest regions, I pray that the fates will be kind to you — may victory be yours in battle, and may fortune find you! Remember always that adversity is only a part of that thing we call adventure — so do not falter in the quest that drives you. Carry on unstoppably toward your destination, and never forget to enjoy the path along the way.

Last, friend, I will leave you with this thought: It may be that we shall meet one day in this world, perchance in the taverns of Galliene, or on a ship bound for the high seas, or maybe somewhere pleasant in the field or the forest. I will in the meantime be wandering this landscape upon a voyage of my own, so until then, bold traveler, be well!

Your humble scribe,

Ben Boos